August

Also by Maryann D'Agincourt

Journal of Eva Morelli

All Most

Glimpses of Gauguin

Printz

Shade and Light

August

Maryann D'Agincourt

PP
Portmay Press
New York

Cover image: *Bordighera*, 1884, Claude Monet (1840–1926), oil on canvas, Potter Palmer Collection, Art Institute of Chicago.

Cover design and book layout by Emily Albarillo
Printed in the United States of America
First printing, 2021

ISBN 978-1-7360536-2-1 (hc)
ISBN 978-1-7360536-3-8 (pb)
ISBN 978-1-7360536-4-5 (ebook)

Library of Congress Control Number: 2021908951

Publisher's Cataloging-In-Publication Data
(Prepared by The Donohue Group, Inc.)

Names: D'Agincourt, Maryann, author.
Title: August / Maryann D'Agincourt.
Description: New York : Portmay Press, [2021]
Identifiers: ISBN 9781736053621 (hardcover) | ISBN 9781736053638 (paperback) | ISBN 9781736053645 (ePub)
Subjects: LCSH: Honeymoons--Italy--Riviera--Fiction. | Widows--Fiction. | Husbands--Fiction. | Family secrets--Fiction. | World War, 1939-1945--Fiction. | LCGFT: Domestic fiction.
Classification: LCC PS3604.A332544 A94 2021 (print) | LCC PS3604.A332544 (ebook) | DDC 813/.6--dc23

PP

Portmay Press
244 Madison Avenue
New York, NY 10016
www.portmaypress.com

Dedicated to Carmela Millie Coscia,
dear godmother and guiding inspiration

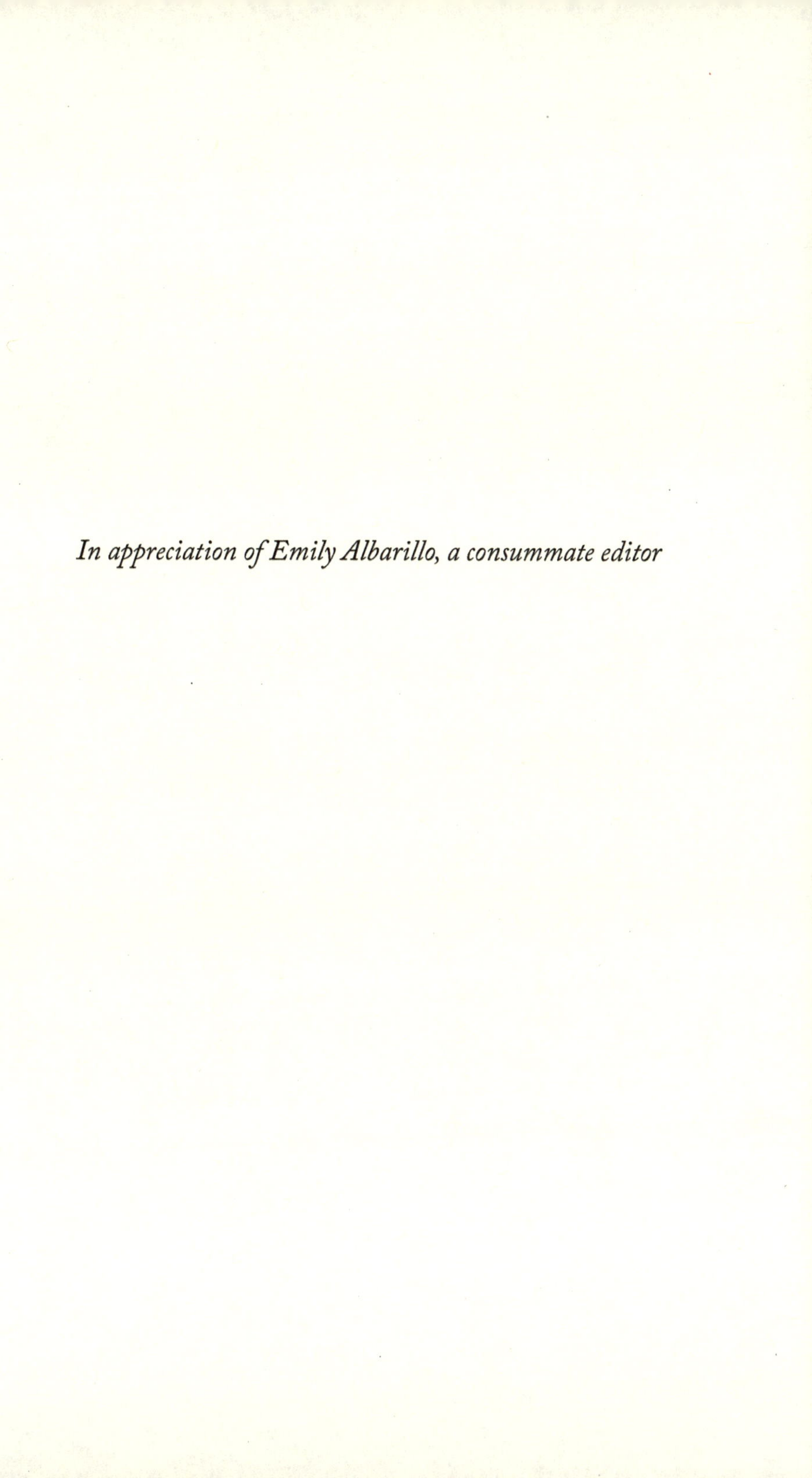

In appreciation of Emily Albarillo, a consummate editor

We looked at the venerable stream not in the vivid flush of a short day that comes and departs for ever, but in the august light of abiding memories.

—Joseph Conrad, *Heart of Darkness*

Prologue

Those early years are hazy and unfocused in memory, pale brushstrokes of a newly begun painting. Through the lens of time you recall a silk-like scarf draped over the arm of an unfinished chair, a necklace with a stone, the shape and color of which you strain to envision, resting on the bony chest of a woman whose face is a blank, an inkling of a stain on the rug near the door. Images lacking the distinctness of firm color, pressed against your dim recollection of the first apartment you lived in with your parents—you were too young to perceive more, to fill in forms and hues.

Of the Saturday soirees in August, the month your mother and father entertained, you only are aware of what you were later told. Reminiscing, their expressions ponderous, they would say how hot and close it was—over fifty people crowding together, conversing, while from the record player, opera—most often Aida *and the voice of Caruso—resounded throughout the room. Your father then would cross his narrow, firm legs and clear his throat, and your mother, her ankles touching, her shoulders erect, would raise her eyes as if to inspect the ceiling; in a pensive and respectful way they'd speak, in near unison, of Giorgio, a former colleague of your father's, engineers during the pre-war days of Europe. They described him as small-framed and thin, his hair and mustache thick and full, overpowering in contrast to his lithe physique. Whenever the heat became oppressive, Giorgio rolled up his sleeves, unbuttoned his shirt, and thrust open a window; sitting on the ledge, gripping the sill with his small hands, he leaned forward to catch a breeze, his legs dangling against the side of the four-story building. Some would laugh with excessive delight, their faces flushed from wine or alcohol, while the sober ones expressed their unease.*

One night, Giorgio, his head bowed, asked to sleep on their sofa, explaining that his wife was away, visiting family in Venice. When your parents awakened the next morning, there was no trace of him; vanished, your mother added with emphasis. They would never see him again. It was assumed though not verified that he had joined his wife in Italy. Not concluding their story of Giorgio, your parents said no more. They sat back in their roomy chairs and looked into the distance, as if gazing across the rough, blue Atlantic, then in to the world of their pasts.

Their guests, immigrants mostly from Trieste, like themselves, had left Europe following the war. Later, in the next apartment where there were no parties, friends and acquaintances from past days occasionally would visit on a Sunday afternoon, some of them smoking heavily, a few with pronounced shadows beneath their eyes. Their smiles revealed a range of emotions, from unflinching wariness to pure contentedness. Over time you gleaned that they had been shaken from the misplaced loyalties in their country of origin; they had come to America to forget, to start anew, to regain their composure.

You left Hartford a month short of your fourteenth birthday. In the back seat of the car, shoes off, knees raised, your hand grazing the vinyl material of the cushion, your parents silent in the front. From the radio you heard the news, the reader's words at times sounding staticky, more often soft and distant. It was March 1968, and like your visual memories, your auditory ones are vague as well, a faint word here and there, often repeated, not seeming to connect to the next one—"Warsaw"; "King"; "North Vietnamese." Words you heard from time to time during those years, words that elicited a distant confusion as if you were living beneath low gray clouds that might never disperse.

Your mother wore brown that day, and the zipper of her dress was not fully up; the back of her neck was full, freckled and protruding. You cannot recollect how she appeared when she turned to ask if you were hungry or thirsty, or what your father's expression was either—all you remember are his steely and darting eyes, peering into the rearview mirror. You sensed they were ambivalent about the move to the outskirts of Boston.

What was most clear was that you were leaving behind a particular place in your Hartford bedroom. You inhabited it and so it had become an extension of you, of where you chose to hide. It was next to the window, from where, sitting on the hardwood floor, you would stretch your neck and view the activity on the street below, a radiator beneath the sill. You'd sit and often read, believing it was your territory where you could view, imagine, and learn about the planet. You felt empowered. You kept close a book with a map of the world, and oftentimes, spreading out two fingers, you would place one on Europe and the other on North America, straddling both continents, the blue Atlantic in between. You belonged in both places, but not by choice. In this small space you experienced a sense of order, an inner contentment that evaporated once you stood up and mustered the determination needed to walk away.

One

The Postcard

Summer, 1984. A wet June evening, the rain strong and heavy, falls in spurts, flooding the windshield, blinding our view; my second husband and I, driving north, pass the sign to Hartford. Up ahead there's been an accident; Jonas presses the brake. In profile, his face appears longer, more angular; the hollows in his cheeks not tempered by the round turn of his chin. Lights flash and a policeman in bright rain garb, directing traffic, signals for us to move forward. On the side of the road, close to the ambulance, a woman sits on the curb, her legs extended, her face pale, her features undefinable. I see no more; we have passed the scene.

The glistening road and frenetic movement of the wipers draw me to an image, a memory of a man wearing charcoal-colored pants. His step was long and brusque, the fabric clung to his legs; my head parallel to his kneecap, my bare feet nestled into a warm rug. A woman whose face was unrecognizable sat in a chair against the wall, her legs spread, a red stain on her lap. Neither frightened nor angry, I watched the man walk swiftly past her; I was deeply aware that this moment, in one form or another, would always be with me.

Though the rain is now a soundless drizzle, the traffic on the highway remains heavy; we make several stops along the way. The drive from our apartment in New York to my mother and father's home outside of Boston takes longer than usual.

Past midnight, we pull into the driveway. Quietly, we let ourselves in with the key I've kept for the past twelve years. We tiptoe past my parents' bedroom, go down the short hallway, and into the room that once was mine.

Unable to sleep, I replay the unearthed memory in my mind. Jonas shifts his lean and wiry body; his back to me, I run one finger down then up and across his skin as I would as a child on the beach after the tide receded, drawing lines in the moist, firm sand. While the adults were embroiled in conversation, anticipating the long drive back to Hartford, I would lower my head, my heart beating fiercely, and touch my face to the wet sand. Then I'd run to the sea to wash it off; the muddy weight of it pressing my cheeks and forehead.

The next day is bright and clear, the midday sun glinting over the surface of the automobile; we drive toward the ocean and a mild breeze caresses us. My parents are in the back seat, their expressions stoic in different ways.

We dine at a restaurant across from the shore, with an encompassing view of the Atlantic, the windows open, light streams in; we linger over our lunch. As a party of four passes our table, a shadow crosses my father's high forehead. He wears a tan-colored shirt, his complexion appearing less gray. Fully engaged in our cursory discussion of politics, his responses are exacting, practical, yet his eyes reflect disquietude, more so than usual. My mother is dressed in a yellow-gold dress, a large onyx ring tight on her second finger. She is animated today, buoyed by the glare of the sun.

I lean forward and announce that in August we plan to take a belated honeymoon, that we are looking for a place near water; Jonas hopes to sketch, I say, then take a sip of coffee.

"Are you considering Trieste, Jenny? Jonas?" my mother suggests, sounding more ambivalent than encouraging; her hand outstretched, her palm upward, she taps the stone of her ring against the table. Bemusedly she eyes my father, her lips part, the lower one quavering; he signals for the waitress, and orders a second martini.

Later we visit Jonas's mother, Cora; she opens her front door, appears preoccupied as she greets us. Though once seated, her legs crossed, her pants cut just above her ankles, she intently studies Jonas, then me. Gradually her gaze becomes less and less penetrating, her eyes drift away, now focusing on the wall behind us; perhaps a photograph of Jonas as a young boy has caught her attention. Petite, her movements concise, her presence is never burdensome—as if her purpose in life is not to oppress. Her half smile is sweet and ironic, like Jonas's; it reveals they are mother and son. Her erect form is softened by the late afternoon light.

Lowering her eyes, she speaks of a possible vacation; she's thinking of driving north, into Canada, maybe Montreal. Montreal, a city that reflects who she is—small, intricate, active, never overbearing. Alternately, she taps each forefinger on her lap, debating, it seems, opposing viewpoints in her mind. Is she considering traveling with Harold, her partner of many years, whom she rarely mentions, and with whom Jonas is minimally acquainted? Despite her restiveness, she is, invariably, steady. For Cora's natural warmth, quietly expansive, supersedes her innate sense of order and moments of preoccupation; a woman whose husband unexpectedly passed away prior to his deployment to a world war and birth of their only child.

Before dinner, my mother, her cheeks flushed from the warmth of the stove, serves each of us an aperitif. With glass in hand I go into the bedroom to look for a book I left behind the last time we visited, a biography of Caravaggio. After perusing the volumes on the shelf without success, I place my drink on top of the desk.

Half listening to the muted conversation between Jonas and my parents coming from the living room, I open the bottom drawer and notice Roth's *Goodbye, Columbus.* With bemusement—for now it would not capture my interest—I pick it up. Holding it, I dismissively flip through the novella. But soon, lodged between two pages of the book, I discover a postcard. With no recollection of having received it, I hold the card up to the fading light; on the front is a picture of a large and uninspiring hotel overlooking a glistening Mediterranean Sea. The edges of the card are still firm and the face of it as glossy as it must have been the day it was sent, though the angle of the picture and the quality of the paper suggest it is not from the present. When I turn the card to the other side, my heart thumps erratically. For the slanted signature is that of my late, first husband, Eric Stram; the date on the card is August 1, 1972. His letters are close, difficult to read. At the time I did not know him well. He did not mention that he hoped to visit me soon; it was a superficial greeting from an acquaintance.

For over a decade the novella and card have lain untouched in the bottom drawer of the desk in this bedroom where I spent the last four years of my youth. Over my eighteenth summer, I read *Goodbye, Columbus* three times, and Lawrence's *Women in Love* once. I was drawn to both because each work introduced me to a concept that for the most part was foreign—one of unabashed freedom.

The voices of my mother, father, and husband sound more distant now, as if coming not from the present but from years ago, and it is not the polite but reserved exchange they share with Jonas; instead it is as if they are with Eric, and I imagine their speech as intense and rapid, how it was whenever they conversed with my first husband. I put the book back into the drawer, and with postcard in hand I stare out the window at the growing twilight through which the passing cars appear to move in slow motion. Abruptly realizing I should join my parents and Jonas, I tuck the postcard in the back pocket of my blue jeans, pick up my glass, and walk out of the room, closing the door behind me.

August light, golden yet muted, falls through the open bedroom window, circling the edges of the beveled mirror frame. I lean across the bureau, my weight on my wrists, gauge my reflection in the glass; with purpose, I say, "I was Jenny Smila until I became Jenny Stram; now I am Jenny Smila-Hoffman—yet I am not a name." From time to time in the same spot I will speak this sentence. The words are a prayer of sorts, a mantra, a means of calming and centering myself, replacing the time and space in my Hartford bedroom where I was content.

Lowering my gaze, I follow an amorphous shadow crossing the surface of the bureau; the long step of the man with clinging charcoal-colored pants comes again to mind. My awareness has grown, but of what I am not certain.

At the window, my fingers press the sill; our third-floor apartment overlooks a small grassy area. Peering out into the morning heat, my gaze settles on Jonas. Below, beneath a willow tree, he sits with his knees raised, his eyes assess the sketchpad resting against his narrow thighs, languidly he fingers the grass, the supple branches loop over him like dangling beads.

Looking upward, warm air grazes my forehead. The sky is pale, nearly clear. In the mellow light, wisps of white clouds reflect the caressing nature of the morning. Jonas sketches, but then suddenly stops and rests his head against the bark. His mind is off somewhere. And watching how he slightly frowns, it strikes me that the two years and seven months of our marriage have been almost seamless; this thought pricks me like an insect bite, piercing and sweet. My realization of the passing of this time and that I do not feel closer to Jonas causes the initial sting. But there is a subtle pleasure in my recollection as well; I am more fulfilled, more independent than I've ever been.

Now sketching again, his hand moves across the pad, the other one holding down the sheet. Although we had been neighbors for four years, it was not until my eighteenth summer that Jonas and I, over the gate separating our backyards, first spoke. As I approached, he tightened his grip on the art pad in his left hand. Hungry fingers, I thought, and later I would realize whenever he sketched or painted he would do so with a devouring intensity, as if with each stroke in some way he was feeding both the active hand and the passive one.

One cool evening last April, we walked after dinner; the sky was clear, the stars visible between the skyscrapers. Turning onto Seventh Avenue, Jonas, his smile fading, described, as he has in the past, his initial impression of me, his fourteen-year-old new neighbor, sitting in the shade beneath the garage roof in her backyard. How I had reminded him of a young woman in Botticelli's painting *Primavera*. And how, he musingly added, very soon afterward he'd moved out to San Francisco and did not see me again until we first spoke. Then a strong brief wind, reminiscent of March, rattled us, and we stopped walking; he held me close, an expression of anxiety—or was it passion—flickered across his face.

I wondered if he prefers the shadowy and painted versions of me. When we returned to our apartment, he closed the door behind us, and grasped my arm, our mouths and bodies pressing together.

Jonas had misgivings about my marriage to Eric Stram. I know because I understand him, his biases. I also believe he was saddened by Eric's death. Yet there is a part of my past of which Jonas is unaware. In the rushing fog of my first marriage I eventually understood in order for the mist to clear I needed to loosen myself from my relationship with my husband. Jonas was my first choice, though I knew he would not be interested; I was married. But at the time I was determined, more than I consciously realized, to find solace from someone else, even a stranger.

During our years in New York, Eric and I frequented a travel agency on Madison Avenue. The agent we'd worked with was a fatherly looking man with fine red hair and soft green eyes. When I walked into the agency office last month, a sweltering July afternoon, he was the only one at his desk. It took him a few minutes to recall I was a former customer of his. He asked after my husband; instead of answering, I reached across the desk and presented him with the postcard I'd found in the book. He studied it for a while, then an expression of recognition crossed his face. With confidence he said the hotel straddles the French and Italian Rivieras, and that the colors of the foliage in the area are marvelous. Immediately, I decided this is where we would spend our belated honeymoon, and promptly asked him to book it from August second to the thirtieth. My rationale was that it would be a good place for Jonas to sketch.

When I returned home, I went directly to our bedroom, pulled open the drawer of the night table, and placed the postcard inside.

I now hear Jonas jiggling his key into the lock of the door, and go out to meet him. Unshaven, his expression is dark, studied, and I think of the image of Caravaggio, from a self-portrait, on the cover of the biography. He places his sketchpad on the counter. Then he draws me close. "Have we waited too long?" he asks. There is a tension in his long face; his eyes search mine.

"It is as good a time as any, and the heat in New York is oppressive in August," I answer, my voice sounding strained; I avoid his gaze. "We should start packing," I add, heading toward the bedroom. He comes up behind me and gently tugs my ponytail.

I pull my nightgown up and then over my head. "How I detest packing," I say, tossing the negligee onto the bed.

"Let's try to make it not too dull," he responds, and his voice sounds far away but he is close; his hands, reassuring, cup my breasts.

* * *

The taxi arrives outside our building at 5 p.m. Jonas carries the suitcases down the winding stairway. Following him, I hesitate before closing the door of the apartment; turning away, I go back inside the bedroom and pull open the drawer of the night table. I take out the postcard, study the picture, and then Eric's writing on the back. I slip the card inside the front pouch of my tote bag.

Two

The Hotel

From a distance I glimpse the hotel; it is situated on a rocky hill bordering the Italian and French Rivieras. As we drive closer, Jonas abruptly changes gears of the Fiat. The building is a formidable yet odd structure, made more so by how incongruous it appears in contrast to the extraordinarily beautiful surroundings; I gaze up at it with mingled feelings of dread and hope. The road is narrow and winding and after a sharp turn our view is momentarily blocked. Now, directly approaching the hotel, it is evident that the facade is postmodern, veering toward a semicircular shape, with a steel and concrete exterior. Magenta-colored bougainvillea and palm trees cover the lower front of the structure; a short distance away, in its sparkling splendor, lies the deep blue Mediterranean.

We park near the entry. Jonas hands the key of the car to the valet, a thin and energetic man with a deep and solemn tan, and then we carry our suitcases up a circular marble stairway. It's a strikingly hot afternoon, and our climb is slow and uneven. I stop for a moment and hold on to the banister. Jonas has reached the top step. He looks over and our gazes meet; though there is uncertainty in his eyes, his smile is broad and firm.

In a daze from lack of sleep, we step inside the lobby, paved with marble and decorated with bronze and marble sculptures; intricate, richly colored paintings; and tapestries. Brocade sofas and chairs and large gold-framed mirrors adorn the interior. In the far corner is a baby grand piano. I have not been here before, but the interior is remarkably familiar; my thoughts stray to my other honeymoon.

We did not sleep the night following our wedding; the party after the ceremony had continued until the next morning. In the early afternoon, we said good-bye to our family and friends surrounded by their luggage in the hotel lobby. There was the group from Trieste and another from the United States. Eric was gracious and humble with the departing guests, clearly enunciating each of their names, thanking them for coming. Though I'd not observed this side of him before, I'd been told he had an uncanny ability of remembering people's names, even those he'd met only once and had not seen for five or more years.

Once the guests left, Eric decided to take a walk, and I went up to our suite to shower and change. It was a warm afternoon in early September and from the window I noticed the sky had a golden hue to it; autumn was approaching. After I showered, I went into the bedroom and found Eric lying naked on the bed, sound asleep. I went over to him; there was a hard whiteness to his skin tone I had not before registered. Inwardly I was alarmed; I had no desire to touch him. Then, as if feeling my presence, he opened his eyes and looked over at me, his blue-gray gaze catching mine. Reflexively I stepped back. He patted the side of the bed, raised his brows, and said, "Come lie next to me, Jenny."

Uneasy now, my heart beats rapidly, as if I expect Eric to walk into the lobby, his head slightly lowered. He'd wear a pressed white shirt, short-sleeved, and dark blue pants; the light coming through the open French doors would accentuate his blond-brown hair, unruly despite his overall neat appearance; he'd efficiently shake Jonas's hand, make a comment about my dress—very bright. His expression would be impassive, then he'd smile to signal his words were meant as a compliment.

For a time I fully believed it would not have angered him if I had another love interest, that he might have preferred it.

Now Jonas's sleepy eyes roam the lobby, rest in the direction of a marble sculpture of a white fawn; languidly he moves toward it, soundly bringing me to the present.

From the balcony of our hotel room, there is an expansive view of the Mediterranean. In silence, Jonas and I lean against the railing, stare out, awed by the majesty of the sea. A light breeze ruffles the flags in the courtyard below. After a while, almost in unison as if drunk from beauty, we turn away and pass through the sliding glass door and back into the room. Slowly, as if in a dream, we lift our luggage onto the bed and begin to unpack.

Sunlight streams into the room, illuminating Jonas's high forehead and shoulders, encircling his long waist. His voice, as angular as his face, sounds stilted and tired; opening his suitcase, he says, "The sea—breathtaking—and so is the color of the bougainvillea. The exterior of the building is utilitarian—functional, practical. But our room, the balcony, the view is magnificent." Lowering his head more, he begins to remove his clothing from the case.

Yet I am compelled by the contrast between the ugliness of the exterior structure and the grandeur of the sea, the beauty of the foliage and the sophistication of the finer works of art. The dichotomy allows me to feel settled, confident—perhaps elevated.

In a chaise longue, one arm dangling, my fingertips graze the hot grains of sand; hazily I look out at the Mediterranean. The water appears still, yet sparkles beneath the rays of the sun. Rocks border the sea. It is five in the afternoon. I am a short distance from the shore, surrounded by rows of beach chairs and umbrellas. The sun will not set for a while. Not yet accustomed to the six-hour time change, I find it difficult to accept where I am.

In the distance I spot Jonas on a ledge of rocks, waves cresting a few feet below, a sketchpad resting on his raised knees; with charcoal in hand he frantically draws, perhaps captivated by the movement of the waves or the wings of a seagull. Then he looks upward and stretches out his legs, his head back as if he is soaking up the warmth. His pose is reminiscent of the photo hanging on the wall of his mother's living room; in it, he's lying in the grass, his arm covering his face, as if shielding himself from the warm rays or protecting himself from an onslaught of piercing slashes of rain.

As I try to imagine what Jonas may be thinking, how he might be assessing his work, it occurs to me that I had never attempted to guess what was on Eric's mind, what had intrigued him most about the business he was part of. It would have been impossible to know, I had assumed, because of his experience as a child during the war—horrific, I had gleaned from his nightmares; his thought process to a degree was a disoriented one. I had concluded that what was essential was not what he was thinking about but how he ruminated over what concerned him at any particular moment, and given my paltry knowledge of his past it would have been impossible for me to comprehend, let alone follow.

A child's cry distracts me from my thoughts. Turning in the direction of the sound, I notice a young family, a mother, father, and son lying in beach chairs in the same row as ours, three seats away. The boy, a toddler, is sprawled across the father's naked lean stomach—he has just awakened from a nap and is crying out for a drink. A large beach umbrella open above their chairs protects them from the piercing sun. The mother abruptly sits up, then stands, wiggling her feet inside her sandals; with two fingers of each hand she efficiently adjusts the shoulder straps of her bathing suit and then makes her way to the refreshment stand. As she places her order, her words are not easily audible, but soon I realize she is speaking French.

Wincing, she thrashes through the hot sand toward her family, and then hands the glass bottle to her husband. He sits up in his chair, loosens the child from his chest, pours the liquid into the paper cup he's pulled from a knapsack, and then presses it to his son's mouth. The little boy, his face a feverish red, his dark eyes large and tired, takes quick fast gulps, and then moves his head away to indicate he has had enough. There is something about the mother that is familiar—strong yet wavering, very dark eyes, exotic.

Lying back in the lounge chair, shading my eyes with one hand, I see Jonas approaching. Once our gazes meet, we both half smile. Soon he is lying in the chair next to mine. His eyes are closed, his sketchpad on his lap. I feel his hand reach for mine. Clasping Jonas's hand, I shut my eyes tightly. Searching my memory for the person who resembles the French woman, my thoughts wander from the French and Italian Rivieras and Eric's Mediterranean business trips, while I stayed alone in the summer heat of New York City, to seven years ago, and then almond-shaped brown eyes. I recall her inquisitive and detached look, and how as she had introduced herself vigorously had shaken my hand.

I had told her my name was Jenny Stram. We'd been lingering under a store awning on Madison Avenue. It was a steamy July afternoon, and we were waiting for a heavy downpour to subside. We stood with our arms crossed and listened to the steady rain drum against the top of the awning; at first we spoke sparingly. After five minutes of small talk, we cautiously began to converse.

I guessed she was in her early fifties, close to my mother's age. She wore a sleeveless white dress, an A-line style, that fell three or four inches past her knee. Her arms and face were tanned. She was of average height, her shoulders broad, her ankles slim. Her eyes were an exotic shape, a deep brown color, her chin narrow for her face. She peered at me and asked what type of work I did, her voice both curt and warm. I explained that my husband and I had not been living in New York long, and I was trying to decide on a career, that I was taking courses, hoping to discover a field that would suit me. I added that I had just completed a course in journalism and was considering taking another one in the fall. This was when she enthusiastically shook my hand and introduced herself as Isa Sokolov. She said she had a connection with someone who was a professor of journalism at a small college outside of the city. She said she would call and see if this professor would talk with me, help steer me in a particular direction. Before we parted that afternoon, we agreed to meet two days later, on Saturday morning.

Eric had told me he would return from his business trip on the following Sunday afternoon. Over the nearly three years of our marriage, I had learned to assume that Eric's definition of business could possibly mean personal as well as professional. We were not estranged as a couple but nearly so. He came and went as he pleased and I had not yet decided how I would go about doing so as well. Though I had disliked admitting it, I'd been hoping that we were only experiencing another phase in our marriage and that eventually we would become closer.

I met Isa at a coffee shop close to our Midtown apartment. She seemed different this day. Two days before she had been wearing a dress and her face had been made up; eyeliner and lipstick had been applied with great care. On this day she was dressed in tight blue jeans and a mauve-colored, V-neck T-shirt. Her manner was different as well. I attributed her casual appearance to the rising heat; it was eleven o'clock in the morning, early to be meeting on a Saturday at the height of summer. But it had been her choice to get together at this time.

In the sharp morning light, her features appeared more harsh, her chin pointy rather than narrow. She seemed unsettled, not composed as she had two days before. We sat outside; although the sun was strong, the temperature had not yet reached its peak. She wore large dark glasses; whenever she questioned me, she would remove her shades, smile abruptly, her eyes squinting, and then put them on again.

My family name was Smila, I told her, and I'd lived in Hartford until I was fourteen. When I asked if she'd ever been there, she shrugged, did not remove her dark glasses, and with a tight smile said she could not keep track of where she'd been.

She lit a cigarette and attempted to speak evenly but there was a hoarseness in her voice, "You are young and beautiful; your life is before you." Her mouth was set, her facial expression was fixed, her lips pursed; tension crossed her forehead.

Continuing, she said, "My hope had been to become a translator—I am fluent in Italian, French, and Russian," she brusquely explained. "But I fell in love with the man who offered to hire me, and decided to decline the position. There were two reasons: the first of course is that we had become involved—I would have felt uncomfortable;

there would have been gossip, and secondly, I did not think I would be suited to a career in translation. A few years later I married someone else."

Before I had a chance to respond, a man came up behind her and rested his hands on her shoulders. He was quite tall, even taller than Eric, and I thought he might be five to ten years older than Isa. She turned her face to him, her voice abrupt, and said, "You startled me, darling." But she did not appear surprised to see him. As I got up to leave, she held up her hand as if to stop me. "Jenny Smila Stram, I'd like you to meet Hans, Hans Sokolov." I shook his hand; his fingers were long and thin, more narrow than mine. Then neither of them spoke, but looked away, as if to indicate my time with them was over. There was an evident tension between them. I walked home feeling disoriented by the change in her personality and that she had not mentioned whether or not she had called her contact on my behalf.

When Eric returned the next day I told him about my encounter with Isa and Hans Sokolov. It was another close, hot day. I did not want to ask about his business trip—he'd been in Chicago the past week—for I knew he would not be direct with me; he would evade my questions, speak cryptically about his work. I was in no mood for that.

But ever since our wedding three years before, I had begun to put the pieces together and realize it wasn't Eric's own business; he worked for a prominent person whose headquarters, once in Philadelphia, was now in Europe. Eric would travel the world, but mostly throughout the United States, to do his bidding.

Eric sat opposite me, his legs resting on the ottoman; he smiled loosely, listened carefully and with interest to what I was saying. When I finished speaking he responded readily, "Oh, yes, Isa and Hans Sokolov—I met them about five years ago and have seen them from time to time in passing since we have come to New York. But I do not know if they remember me. I was on a business trip, staying at a hotel on the Riviera, the Italian side. I found them to be an interesting couple; yes, she was an interesting woman. It was before you and I became involved, of course." Then he smiled in that haunting way of his, and said, "I believe she may be from Trieste. What a small world it truly is, Jenny."

I still feel Jonas's grip on my hand and soon doze off. When I open my eyes, I am uncertain how long I've been sleeping. There is a light breeze now. My eyes are blurry and I realize Jonas is no longer holding my hand. I feel his absence but hear his voice; following the sound of it, I look over and see he is conversing with the French family. The woman's expression is no longer stern; she throws back her head and laughs at whatever Jonas is saying in his halting French. I look past them to the front of the hotel; from this angle the foliage is not visible, I only see the steel and concrete exterior.

Three

The Guests

Evenings, before dinner, guests drift into the grand lobby to listen to the pianist. Freshly showered after a day spent bathing, sightseeing, or cycling beneath the piercing sun, they lounge on brocade sofas and chairs, dressed in informal yet well-pressed clothing, sitting upright, legs crossed, ears cocked in the direction of the musician. Clutching a glass of chardonnay or Campari, they reach for tiny hors d'oeuvres from the full plates the white-jacketed waiters have placed on low tables before them. Conversations, as they tend to be in the early evening hours, are tempered, almost listless.

The pianist, in his late thirties, dressed in a black tuxedo and cream-colored shirt without a tie, the top button open; his expression is both alert and melancholic, his eyebrows fine semicircles. His shoulders rise gracefully, soulfully as he plays a Duke Ellington or Johnny Mercer song, occasionally one favored by Sinatra or Bennett. From time to time he'll sing one of these melodies—always in French, yet his name is Italian. He is referred to as Mr. Poldini. At 9:30 p.m., each night, ninety minutes before he is finished for the evening, he'll erupt into a classical piece—Beethoven's *Moonlight Sonata* or a Chopin polonaise. By then some of the guests will have returned to listen. They will have come into the lobby after having enjoyed a satisfying dinner outside on the patio, the Mediterranean not far away, having been serenaded by the swishing sound of the waves while mildly aware of the dim lights in the courtyard surrounding the pristine pool and the flags from various countries on tall poles, colorful, inanimate guards.

Sitting away from the pianist, but with a clear view of him, we listen to his rendition of a series of Ellington's songs. Intermittently I feel the pressure of Jonas's arm against my shoulder. Mr. Poldini plays in a precise almost staccato-like way, never exuberantly, more respectful of the notes and melody.

Jonas's studied gaze wanders over to the other guests and settles on the man and woman sitting next to an antique harp; the instrument is at an angle behind the piano. They appear to be in their late twenties, early thirties. The woman is dressed slightly more casually than the other patrons. They are British—earlier I had walked by the concierge desk and had overheard them inquiring about the afternoon tea hour, adding that they are Londoners. He is dressed in a white short-sleeved shirt and dark pants, he has a narrow face and wide, flat forehead, his small blue eyes following those passing through the foyer. She has short red hair with bangs and is wearing black jeans and high-heeled shoes, a thin gold chain round her left ankle. Her face lights up and she raises her eyebrows in an abstract disbelief whenever Mr. Poldini plays a complicated sequence of chords. She often looks over at her companion with obvious concern—but his demeanor is closed, unreadable. I wonder how Jonas sees them. Maybe he would like to draw the woman, I think, attempt to capture her sense of wonder.

Jonas turns to me; in his eyes I see a look of gratification tinged with irony.

When we go outside to the patio, the maître d', dressed in a dark jacket and pants, approaches us; there is a smoothness in his step, a keen expression in his eyes, a practiced intent to display his confidence, his professionalism. He shows us to a table. As he holds out the chair for me I hear in the distance the lulling sound of lapping waves. There is a very slight breeze, and I draw a light shawl across my shoulders.

After the waiter has taken our order, I ask Jonas if he'd like to sketch the woman who was sitting close to the harp. "No," he says, surprised by my question. Then he smiles. "I would choose to draw the man next to her." Half smiling, he continues, his voice uneasy, "Jenny, there are straightforward people who for the most part are as they appear and there is nothing wrong with that; it actually is refreshing. But there are those who are opposite to what they seem. I never know for certain, but as I sketch, it slowly becomes clear."

He often expresses such thoughts; it is as if he has turned them over in his mind, questioning, then reaffirming his approach. His words reveal his humanness, his humbleness, but there are instances when he is not this way, when he is less accessible; at these moments I am reminded of the haunting image of Caravaggio on the cover of the biography.

I gaze up past a trellis of flowers and see on the closest balcony a woman alone, in her late thirties, wearing a strapless black dress, leaning against the railing, her arms outstretched, her head back, her hair falling long past her shoulders, looking quite comfortable; I wonder if she comes to this hotel every August, and if so had she met or passed

Eric in the foyer or walking along the beach. My mind wanders to the postcard he sent twelve years ago. When I discovered it in June, I only glanced at his words. They seemed devoid of any particular meaning, hastily written; perhaps he had felt obliged to send me a note. I was more intrigued by the photo of the hotel on the front of the card. By deciding to come here I may have been hoping to unlock the mystery of Eric in some way, what he refrained from telling me, what I never asked. I believe he was last at this hotel four or more years ago; yet the environment appears as uncomplicated as a person my husband would not be compelled to sketch or paint.

The scraping of chairs disrupts my thoughts. I look across the table but Jonas does not return my gaze; he is absorbed in watching whatever is happening at the table behind me. I hear voices, an argument. A younger woman speaks assertively and then I hear an older woman's voice, hoarse and raspy, her words slurred and loud. Two men respond in cajoling voices as if attempting to calm her. I cannot tell if they are all speaking in French or Italian; they may be going back and forth between the languages.

"Jonas," I say in a low voice. "What is it?" He doesn't respond; his expression is brooding. His comprehension of spoken French is better than mine.

"I am not certain, Jenny."

My curiosity aroused, I turn round swiftly, pretending to look for the waiter, and catch sight of the French family I noticed on the beach the day we arrived—the child is not at the table, but there is an older man, and a woman, perhaps in her late fifties. The older woman's presence is harsh and familiar. I shiver and turn to Jonas.

The waiter moves toward us with grace, yet a concerned expression crosses his face. He places our meals before us. Jonas smiles sheepishly, our gazes lock, and he shrugs his shoulders. And I forget about the party behind us until I hear a loud scream, then a shuffling of feet. Now silence. Jonas leans forward and tells me the two men have escorted the older woman away; they have gone up the path behind me. When I turn round and look, I only see the brick walk and velvet green bushes.

After dinner, instead of going inside the lobby to listen to the pianist, we return to our room and sit out on the balcony. From the patio below, we hear the clatter of plates and the sound of the waves, rushing now, and faint piano music issuing from the grand lobby and through the open doors.

I again ask Jonas about the French family, whether he understood what was happening. He is staring straight out at the sea, his profile straight; yet he sits sideways as if evading any anguish he may feel. Not looking at me, he says calmly, rationally, "The older woman was obviously drunk. She was criticizing Helen, the French woman I met on the beach, telling her she had gained weight, that she was not careful enough with her child, that she should have not left him with a babysitter she did not know. When Helen tried to explain, the woman screamed, drowning out Helen's words. Then Helen's husband and the older man escorted her away."

The lights from below half cover his face, causing him to look sterner on one hand and more mellow on the other. Is he thinking of what occurred between Helen and the older woman, or is he pondering how his life would have been different if he had known his father, if he hadn't died from an illness before being deployed to Europe during the Second World War and Jonas's birth, or is he wondering about my marriage to Eric—which I know is a mystery to him? Though he doesn't readily admit it, he can't quite fathom how the young eighteen-year-old Jenny he had known and had regarded as independent-minded could have married the much older and enigmatic Eric Stram.

"Can you hear the music, Jonas?" I ask.

He smiles and says, “Barely. I do not know what he is playing, not even the style—jazz, classical?”

“Yes,” I say, “like something you want to know about a person but can’t quite determine.”

We sit in silence, the moon a thin crescent in the dark sky, surrounded by a multitude of stars.

We soon go to bed. As if lost in a heavy fog, we make love, groping, then surprised by the hardness of each other’s body. Jonas, it seems, is not quite real, more like a shadow with a solid form.

With a start I awake from a horrid dream, the details of it slipping away. Shaken, I strain to recall, but displacing it is the image of the woman with a stain on her lap and the man walking briskly away.

I get up, push aside the long drapes and go out onto the balcony, looking out at the flags in the courtyard, slightly furling from a breeze, then at the Mediterranean, and lastly at the pool below, only partially visible. From the bedroom I hear Jonas’s slow and even breathing.

It is quite beautiful, the sky, a pink-gray color. Dawn is beginning to break, and I hear the quiet, morning cries of the gulls. Leaning over the railing, I spot two folded white towels on the bench close to the pool. The sound of a swimmer treading water is nearly inaudible. A tall distinguished man in a white robe walks by the pool. He must be in his seventies but his step appears younger, energetic. Soon he holds out a towel and wraps it around a woman, a woman of average height, strong, robust. I cannot see her face. But now they are out of my view. It strikes me that they may be the couple who was with the French woman, Helen, and her husband last night.

As I step back into the bedroom, I spot my tote bag on a chair, the gold buckle picking up the light from the rising sun. I grasp the bag; my hand reaches inside the front pouch and I pull out Eric's postcard. I sit down and click on the lamp next to the chair and for the first time I read the message closely.

Greetings from the Riviera, Jenny. It is my first time at this hotel, but expect to be coming more often for business meetings. Met a couple who live in New York and are vacationing here—very nice people. Hope you are enjoying your summer.

Cheers, Eric

A chill runs through me. I look up past the raised foot of the bed and see Jonas stirring in his sleep; he reaches out, expecting to touch me, but his arm falls flat onto the mattress. Does he realize I am absent?

* * *

Out on the patio we eat breakfast; the weather is changing, the sky streaked with a dull light trickling through a gray mist. After we finish our meal, Jonas and I walk toward the center of town. By the time we reach the main street, the sun has fully disappeared behind the clouds. Inside the tourist office, we recognize the British couple we noticed last night in the grand lobby; they are inquiring about other beaches in the area. Once they leave, Jonas leans over the counter and asks for directions to an old castle that is now an art museum; he read about the collection a few weeks ago.

On the street again, a raindrop falls on my arm. Seeing again Eric's handwriting on the postcard has left me uneasy and restless; I tell Jonas I will look about town while he is at the museum. We agree to meet in two hours at the café on the corner across from the tourist office.

I wander in and out of a few shops, one with a large assortment of cheeses, and two with women's clothing. Outside, I look up at the sky; the clouds are heavier and darker now, rain is imminent. I go into a bookstore nearby, choose a novel, an English translation of *Le blé en herbe* by Colette, and then walk to where Jonas and I have planned to meet.

Stepping inside the café, I hear a distant rumble of thunder. I find a seat away from the door. Avoiding the steady gaze of the proprietress who has come to my table, I order an espresso. Then I begin to read the book, the translation is crisp and evocative.

Soon she again approaches my table, her expression both sensitive and commanding. Her white straight skirt and sleeveless top with a scooped neckline reveal her narrow form and accentuate her deep brown tan. With an elegant turn of her wrist she places the cup of espresso on the table. When I look up to thank her, I notice an older man sitting at a table a few feet from mine. I study him carefully and realize he is the man from the pool this morning. He sits facing at an angle away from me. He appears sad, his posture no longer erect, seeming not as confident as he had earlier. He picks up his cup as if moving in slow motion, takes a few exacting sips before placing it down. The beige pants and light blue short-sleeved shirt he is dressed in are well pressed. His white-gray hair is pushed back from his face, emphasizing his high forehead. The proprietress sits across from him and rests her hands on the table. They speak in Italian and I only can pick up a few words. They do not look at each other as they converse; instead they gaze in the direction of the wide entranceway as if waiting for someone to come in.

Within minutes other customers enter. The proprietress goes over to them and in a prompt yet graceful manner takes their orders. When the four or five people have been served, she returns and sits with the man from the hotel. Again they do not look at each other when they speak. But now they converse in English instead of Italian. I am surprised at how fluent they are, and wonder if they lived in an English-speaking country for a period of time. My guess is they do not want to be overheard by the other customers.

They appear more relaxed now that they are speaking in English, though as fluent as they are, it is apparent that it is not their native language. Their voices are low and I can only pick up certain words, enough to recognize the language they are speaking, but not enough to follow the content of their conversation.

They might be married to each other. Then I think uneasily of the other woman at the table last night, who I believe was with him at the pool this morning.

After some time has passed, I take a pause from reading and look up. The man from the hotel is no longer in the café and the other customers have left. The proprietress and I are alone. There is a stillness, a sense of an impending rainstorm.

She comes to my table and asks, her tone sounding preoccupied, if there is anything else I'd like. I answer in English, and she seems surprised. She has forgotten I ordered in a stumbling Italian, that her language was not mine. A startled expression crosses her face, and she frowns. I realize she may be wondering if I overheard her conversation.

There is a close, loud rumble of thunder and then a downpour of rain ensues. She turns her head to the window and when she looks back at me, she appears worried.

"It should pass soon," I say.

She nods, but her expression still shows concern. And I am surprised as she does not seem to be a woman who worries about much; her show of confidence when I first entered the shop has evaporated.

"Your English is quite good," I say, to divert her.

She smiles and I ask her to join me; no other customers will come in until the rain subsides. She sits down, her back to the street and the rain.

"Where are you from?" she pointedly asks. "Are you an American?"

"Yes," I say. "Your English is very good," I repeat.

She smiles demurely. Her hair is a brown-red color; though she is slim, she is strong-looking. Her eyes are small, close, inward, her brows are dark and full, her lips remain partially open whether or not she is about to speak.

"Yes," she says, "it is because my former husband and I lived in Philadelphia for a while. He is a businessman and in the early days he began his enterprise there. He knew many people who came to America after the war. He is not from this area of Italy; he is from Trieste."

Disconcerted that she's mentioned Trieste, I pause to regain my composure, reminding myself that Eric stayed at the hotel in this town, that it is not unusual he would have heard of it from other natives of that city, like himself. I sit silently and wait, not wanting to say words that may affect her mood. For I see she is pondering, not knowing whether or not to speak more. I listen to the sound of the heavy rain, look around her shop at the dainty pastries in the glass case, at the small, round white tables scattered about the interior, the chairs with pink-and-black-cushioned seats.

She turns her head to glance out the window again. And as if the steadiness of the rain has given her confidence to speak, she looks over at me, her eyes, unreadable, and says, "Whenever there is a storm and I see flashes of lightning, I am reminded of all the mistakes I have made over the years. My life has been interesting, but has deviated in many ways. I do not know if deviated is the right word. What I mean is not direct—I have been down many avenues." Her narrow wrist flexing as she moves her hand forward in a meandering way.

She tells me her life on the Riviera was not a pleasant one. "The war," she adds with a detached resignation. She leans in closer and says the man she was talking to over there—she points to the table as if it is significant in some way—was her husband and is no longer. "He fell in love with someone else after we had been married for many years. Although the affair happened much later, I believe it was because of the war. Like him, she was born in Trieste but grew up in America. But he is a good man and we are still close. I am free now, sad but free. And I must admit, I was not an angel either during our marriage. We lived in many places all over the world. He was very successful; he partially retired not too long ago. He owns the big hotel on the Mediterranean."

"It is where I am staying," I say.

She nods. "Most people from other countries stay there because it is beautiful."

"It is beautiful inside," I answer. "The view of the Mediterranean is lovely too."

She smiles and I know she is thinking beyond my words; it is as if I am missing something.

"My former husband bought this café for me. But I only work the last six weeks of summer. I hire others to take care of the shop while I am away. I stay mostly in Paris, where I have an apartment. But I like to travel to other places too. Although I am away most of the year, this café is what keeps me connected to the life and people I knew when I was young. During the weeks I am at the café, my former husband will come every morning for a cappuccino; we talk, sometimes about our past life together, but today we spoke of the present. We will always be connected in one way or another. We spent too many years together as a couple, experienced much pain and much joy. That was until the woman came into our lives. She was staying at the hotel. She knew he was a very wealthy man, owned the hotel. She was married; it was twelve years ago when she and her husband first came. Her name is Isa; as I said, she was originally from Trieste, but lived in the United States since she was a young girl, before the war—that is where she met her first husband. He was Dutch, but had moved to the United States with his family when he was thirteen or so. When they came to stay at the hotel, I immediately liked him much better than her. He was reserved but kind and she was friendly, spontaneous, restive. I'd stay at the hotel with my husband whenever he hosted a business meeting. Naturally I'd have impressions of the guests, sometimes strong ones."

"Do you remember his name?" I ask, sounding more abrupt than questioning.

"Whose name?" she asks.

"The woman you spoke of, Isa, her first husband."

As if compelled by the insistence in my voice, she answers promptly. "Yes, of course. It is Hans. Hans Sokolov."

Four

The Sokolovs

My heart beats rapidly; it was Isa Sokolov who created a scene at the restaurant last night and who I spotted by the pool this morning.

The proprietress's deep-set eyes, sharp and inquisitive, meet my gaze. "Do you know him?" she asks; the lone pearl on her gold chain necklace rises and falls with her breaths.

A week after the July Fourth holiday, ten days before I would meet Isa Sokolov, Eric and I drove to an antique show in Westchester. It was a warm day, the trees were close, the leaves on the oaks a bright green color, the sky faint blue and cloudless. In five days Eric would be attending a meeting in Chicago and in three weeks he would leave for a business trip on the Riviera. Adjusting my hands on the steering wheel, my eyes on the road ahead, I asked about joining him on his upcoming trip to Italy. Then I looked over, caught his puzzled expression, his eyes squinting. He leaned his head back against the cushion and said, "Jenny, why would you want to go to a meeting or see people who would bore you? It is only business." I felt a stab of anger, and began to withdraw any feelings I might have for him. Once Eric left for the Rivera, I concluded it was a relief I had not traveled with him.

The day after Eric left for Europe, I went to the public library for a few hours. I left through the main entrance; walking down the front steps I noticed Hans Sokolov on the sidewalk below. The afternoon heat was intense. His shirt sleeves were rolled up; he was pacing back and forth, from the bottom of the steps to the street corner, dragging the toe of his right foot every time he turned round. His forehead was flat, his nose narrow at the top, broadening at the tip, his cheekbones high and broad, his physique was lean and austere. He reminded me of one of Rodin's sculpted Burghers of Calais. I had been struck by the statue when I had seen it at the Rodin Museum in Paris the previous April.

As I moved toward him, he stopped pacing; placing his hands on his slim hips, he looked over at me, not showing any sign of recognition. I observed again how narrow his fingers were and I thought of Isa and meeting him at the café. I was still bothered by the experience. And although Eric had said he had met Hans and Isa at a hotel on the Riviera about five years before and had run into them a few times since we moved to New York, I concluded after questioning Eric further that he did not know much about them and had been only speaking in that generalized provocative way of his, hinting at things that might not have occurred.

Meeting Isa under the store awning that day was pure coincidence and perhaps she had not recognized my last name, Stram; she might not have remembered Eric. But despite my rationalizations I was unsure. My uncertainty led me to feel on edge; I had hoped to keep the encounter from my mind, especially while Eric was away. Recognizing Hans caused my unease to return, for he was a reminder of how much the episode with Isa Sokolov had disturbed me. Eric's remembering their names without truly knowing the couple had made my brief interaction with them seem more disorienting.

Hans stopped pacing and again looked up the steps of the library, his forehead moist from the heat. In his expression there was a hint of expectancy, his eyebrows slightly raised. Passing him, I studied his profile; it was enhanced by his white-blond hair that he wore longer than most men of his age. His tan had deepened since I had met him ten days before. Raising his hand, he pressed one finger to the side of his face, more in a reserved anticipation than contemplation.

Soon his eyes mildly lit up, like a thirsty child given water rather than the preferred soda to drink. I followed his gaze to see who he had noticed. A rush of people were coming down the steps, but soon approaching him was a man in his early twenties, nearly his height, who appeared as if he might be a younger relation of his. They eyed each other, nodded, not quite in unison, and then began to stroll in the direction of the café where I had met Isa.

Walking in the same direction toward my apartment, I kept a short distance away but was close enough to get a sense of their interaction. At first they did not speak. But after five minutes or so, they began to talk in an intense way. I could not hear their words and did not know if they were in enthusiastic agreement or were having a discussion that would lead to an argument. As I drew closer, I gleaned that they were not in accord with whatever they were discussing. There was a mild tension between them. Walking almost in step, both of them would smile ironically from time to time.

Then I heard a sudden loud screech of brakes. Diverted, I lost sight of Hans Sokolov and his companion and began to walk quickly. At the intersection there was a crowd of people clustered together, and I overheard a man with white hair and wire-rimmed sunglasses mention that either a woman had fainted or been hit by a car. He pointed toward the street. Following the gazes of the other pedestrians, I soon spotted a woman lying prone on the street, a semicircle of onlookers close by.

Hans materialized from nowhere, it seemed; he went over to the woman and crouched next to her, expertly lifting her head onto his lap. With one hand he motioned for the gathered crowd to back away. The man who I thought might be a relative of Hans stood off to the side. Making my way through the crowd, I approached and asked him if he knew what had happened. He didn't take his gaze from Hans, and without looking at me, he pointed to Hans and the woman. He watched closely as Hans administered to her.

When the scene became less frenetic, I caught his attention again and asked if he knew the man who was caring for her.

"It is my father," he said, this time glancing back at me. He shyly caught my gaze.

"He is a doctor?" I asked.

"Yes," he said curtly and turned his gaze back to Hans. I walked away from him but waited until the emergency team arrived and the woman was safely lifted onto the ambulance.

Three days later, walking into the café where I had met Isa, I noticed Hans and his son sitting at a table close to the counter. After Eric had left for the Riviera, I would go once a day to the café, in the late afternoon or early evening; it was relatively close to my apartment. I was not concerned about running into Isa; my intuition was that she would not be there, and if I was wrong, given our last interaction, I was convinced she would ignore me.

I thought Hans's son might be a college student, and assumed he was about twenty years old. I had looked in the telephone book to see what type of doctor Hans was and discovered he had a neurology practice on Park Avenue.

Some time over that summer I had gone to see Jonas at the gallery where he had worked as a portrait artist. Before then, ever since Eric and I had moved to New York, I had seen Jonas four or five times. That day he had appeared more preoccupied with his work than usual; in addition to painting portraits of clients, he was attempting to create his own style of art, which he spoke of at length. Though I believed he was still fond of me, he was more reserved because I had married Eric. I understood it was not possible for Jonas to comprehend my reasons for choosing to do so.

The relentless heat that summer seemed to hover over us, and because of it, the confinement of it, I became more and more intrigued by Hans and his son; they were my sole means of escape. New York was barren, especially during those late weeks of the season. Everything appeared still, my friends were vacationing, and my parents were in Trieste. Though there were tourists, on the whole, the city as it often is during this time of the year was more subdued than usual.

There was no evidence of Isa and that had relaxed me, given me confidence in my ability to assess people. For after a week had passed, I was certain she would not make an appearance—not only because she had not done so, but because her husband and son did not appear to be expecting anyone, and seemed to exist in a private world that only encompassed the two of them.

When Eric returned at the end of the third week of August, he appeared tense. He expressed his anxiety not in an overt way but by withdrawing from any in-depth conversation. He was never unpleasant, just quiet and non-communicative. This tendency of his would always alarm me; I would be fearful of him surprising me with unpleasant news. But whenever I'd catch a glimpse of myself in a mirror, I'd look calm, unruffled, and, for the most part determined. So I imagine he had no idea how much stress I was feeling about his mood. If I had been older and our relationship had been more of a mature one, I would have spoken directly to him about it.

The evening after his return we went out to dinner. Eric made a reservation at a restaurant neither of us had been to before, and he appeared relatively happy; his tenseness had subsided. I felt reassured, though my intention that evening had been to speak with him about our marriage, how I thought the age difference between us was becoming more and more of a strain. It had dawned on me that the precocious attitude I had possessed while I was in college and when I married him at twenty had been factitious. Though I had no proof, I was convinced that Eric had affairs and thought nothing of it. Only fleetingly did it cross my mind that he wanted me to believe this about him, that it might have been an attempt on his part to control me.

At dinner that night he was more attentive than usual, and so I suppressed any thoughts I had of leaving him. I believed he understood I was dissatisfied with our marriage. Until then remaining silent had been my way of asserting myself with him.

He comported himself with his usual easy dignity but, closely studying him as he spoke about a bicycle trip he had taken along the Mediterranean coast, I saw that his blue-gray eyes were more dull than shiny. He had been traveling more than usual at the time and although he was only forty-three, I wondered if it was beginning to take a toll on him. Eric ordered champagne and lobster, attempting to do so as always with a subdued flourish. But he appeared uneasy and sounded halfhearted. When he began to eat, I noticed that although he never had had a large appetite, he ate sparingly while encouraging me to enjoy the meal. My heart beat rapidly; I wondered what he planned to reveal. I attributed his lack of appetite not only to a general fatigue but also to an uncertainty in what he was about to say. For the first time it struck me I held some degree of power over him; I was surprised, though more cautious than emboldened.

He lowered his head, his voice sounded weak, no longer even and provocative. What did I think, he asked, of his living in Europe for a few months? He would be back by late November. I looked directly at him and he avoided my gaze. I understood that he had no intention of asking me to accompany him.

It is because of your work, I responded, attempting to sound nonchalant, sensible. He nodded slowly. Then he clarified, saying it mostly had to do with a specific business deal.

I was torn within. I had not wanted to entirely give up on our marriage, though at times I had acknowledged that I needed to leave him. Yet whenever I had attempted to do so, I had been uncertain, frozen. I half hoped the upcoming break would keep the marriage going, but I realized there was a greater chance this imminent separation could very well be the beginning of the end of it.

"Smile, Jenny," he said in his old way, gliding his head forward; the light from the candle on the table flickering, his blue-gray eyes smoky, "and do finish your lobster—succulent, isn't it?"

The restaurant was on Fifty-Fourth Street, walking distance from our apartment. On our way home, Eric attempted to hold my hand but I avoided his touch. I heard the approaching sound of a police car siren, but did not turn to look as Eric and the other pedestrians had.

When we married three years before, I had been mistakenly convinced that I was the most mature, and that my parents, Eric, and his family, because of the pain they had suffered during the war, which still lingered, existed in a purgatory of sorts that had stunted their growth.

Needless to say I did not interfere with Eric's plan to live in Italy through November, though I imagined it would be longer, as life with him was that way, everything took more time than expected. It was as if part of him was moving through life in slow motion and the other part was active and rushed. It was confusing for me and in a way it was much easier to live a relatively calm life without him.

Eric left on the twenty-sixth of August—he had been home for four days. He seemed more confident during the drive to the airport. He was dressed in a navy blue sports jacket, which brought out the blue in his eyes, the gray more diminished, and a light blue shirt. He seemed completely at ease and assured, the heat not affecting him.

Before he left the car, he leaned over and pressed his lips against each of my cheeks. Smiling, he said, "Take care of yourself, Jenny, do take that course in journalism. It might be a good career for you." But I believed he did not know me well enough to understand what might suit me. Because his life had not been easy, harsh you might say, he invariably attempted to overcome it by viewing people in a superficial way, even those closest to him.

I did not wait to watch the plane take off. Instead I drove back to the apartment building, parked the car in the reserved spot, and then went directly to the café, hoping to see either Hans or his son, just for a sense of solace. For that is what they gave to me—they comforted me without knowing me, the reality of them, that was.

Hans was there, sitting alone, reading a newspaper. He didn't seem to be waiting for anyone. As he riffled through the pages, he appeared concerned, yet his crossed legs and relaxed shoulders conveyed a sense of lethargy. The temperature was not as high as it had been when I had driven Eric to the airport. But his shirtsleeves were rolled up as usual.

It was as if a year had passed since Isa had introduced me to Hans Sokolov. Other than the exotic shape of her eyes, I only vaguely recalled her other features and overall physical appearance; it was her personality that was unnerving, open and perhaps deceptive. I assumed her husband and son were different.

Hans folded the newspaper and got up from his seat. He didn't look around. On his way out, he passed my table and our gazes met; he did not show any sign of recognition. Our introduction had been brief and he and Isa had been so eager to be rid of me he probably had not registered it. He had seemed more preoccupied with Isa, hovering over her, not wanting to be distracted by my presence.

After he left, I lowered my head and opened the book to the page I'd left off reading. I became absorbed by the novel and was unaware of what was happening around me. Soon I heard someone clearing his throat. I looked up and met the earnest gaze of Hans's son.

"Do you mind—there are no other seats available," he said. I nodded.

I resumed reading my book, and he opened his as well. Whenever I glanced up I noticed a slight roundness in his face, a sheen to his skin, an intensity in his blue eyes as he studied the text, then wrote notes; I was convinced I was older than him.

I do not remember which one of us got up to leave first, or at what point he told me his name was Caleb Sokolov, and I do not recall how it came about but by the time I left the café, we had agreed to meet in Central Park the following afternoon.

Before I left my apartment the next day, I reached for the doorknob and noticed the wedding ring on my finger. I stared at it, the late August light flowing in from the window picking up the faint yellow color of the diamond and accompanying rubies. Reflexively, I took it off, uncertain whether or not Caleb had noticed it the previous day.

There were not as many people as usual in Central Park that afternoon. I spotted Caleb before he noticed me. Smoking a cigarette, he appeared uneasy, his body erect as if bracing himself for rejection, perhaps thinking I might not show up. Once he recognized me, he threw down his cigarette, crushing it with his foot.

We walked past the entrance to the zoo. Caleb explained to me that in his last year of high school he had been accepted into an accelerated six-year program that included college and medical training, and I was reminded of how I had accelerated my college classes so I could marry Eric at twenty. Caleb was twenty-two, six months younger than I was. I wondered if he had felt as precocious when he had made the decision at eighteen to become a medical doctor as I had in committing to Eric at that age.

Three days later, we went to a movie. Walking toward the cinema, I was energized; it was as if I had been released from a personal prison. I had still neglected to put on my wedding ring, and since Caleb had not asked about it, I assumed he had not noticed it that day at the café.

When we met in front of the theater, Caleb appeared subdued from the heat. It was the thirtieth of August. The air-conditioning inside the cinema was not effective. While we watched the movie, Caleb reached for my hand, his grasp was an anxious one. Though as he gazed at the movie screen, his demeanor revealed confidence. The movie, a French comedy with English subtitles, was one I had suggested. I thought it would be less provocative than a serious drama or a romantic film.

From time to time Eric would come to mind; I'd wonder where he was. It would have been two in the morning in Europe. Was he walking along the beach, or drinking at a café bar? Randomly I thought how people on the Riviera tend to stay up late, as New Yorkers do, especially on the Italian side; the French towns, unlike Paris, close down earlier.

Caleb sensed my attention was wandering; he lowered his head and asked if I liked the movie, I had withdrawn my hand from his. I nodded and focused again on the film.

Later as we walked in the direction of our apartments, I told him I had enjoyed the movie, even though I had not been in the mood to see a comedy.

"But you were the one who chose it," he said, smiling.

Then he gingerly asked if something was bothering me. And I frantically explained that I was married, that my husband was much older than I was, that I had married him when I was twenty. It had been a mistake to do so, and that I longed to leave the marriage. I told Caleb that meeting him in Central Park and going to the movie with him had been my first steps in doing so. I said I was unsure and certain, both at the same time.

He smiled, but I sensed his disappointment. He paused, then seemed to collect himself, and said that he was patient; that it would be up to me to decide if we were to see each other again, that he was busy with medical school and that he might be in Europe for a while—his father was arranging for him to do an exchange program in Amsterdam for six months.

We stopped for burgers at an all-night diner. The lights were bright and soon we became animated. To an extent, having told him I was married had freed us.

We discussed the movie and we laughed together over certain scenes, but soon there was agitation in our laughter. Caleb's face was red, almost feverish, and my cheeks were burning.

Caleb spoke warmly of his father, and said, as if it were an afterthought, that his mother was in Italy.

We left the diner at three in the morning. More content now, I was wrapped in feelings of stability and happiness and I did not want the mood between us to change. I was elevated; we had bonded, unexpectedly.

What I recall most about our affair were those long afternoons we spent in the apartment while Eric was away, how the late summer sun, then turning to golden autumn light, flowed through the curtains, resting on Caleb's arms and waist. How young he seemed, and how inexperienced he was, but that was what I had relished most about him. He'd stay with me all night—the following day he'd go either to school or the hospital, and return in the evening. He would not mention our relationship to his father, he had said emphatically—he valued privacy.

One morning, at the end of October, the telephone rang; I was still in bed and Caleb was in the shower. It was Eric. His voice sounded distant and somber; he said that he had to go to a meeting in a few minutes and was checking to see if I was well—he'd had a dream about me the night before. I assured him I was fine; I was able to end the call before Caleb came into the room. When he did, he sat close, the palms of his hands pressing the mattress on either side of me; he said he would be free most of the day. I met his gaze, his eyes were the same exotic almond-shape as Isa's, yet the color was like his father's, a Chagall blue. It struck me that in a month he would be in Europe and Eric would be home.

I stroked Caleb's arm and told him that last month a woman had introduced herself as Isa Sokolov; we'd been standing under the awning of a clothing store in the midst of a rainstorm. He did not respond; he studied me as I described our encounter that day and that I had met her again the following Saturday at the café. As I spoke, his eyes never left mine, his hands still on the bed; he remained silent. When I finished speaking, he stood up, lifted the covers and got into bed. It was the only time during our affair he'd been indifferent.

Caleb left at the end of the third week of November, five days before Eric returned. From time to time, he would send me postcards from Amsterdam, signing them with only his initials. We had not made plans to reconnect. Before parting, Caleb and I had met at the café. It was as cold as winter, and the temperature inside the café was low. He grasped my bare hands to warm them, then lowered his gaze and said I needed to make a decision about my marriage. His voice was insistent and firm. And when, after a few months, I did not write to him to say I had decided to divorce Eric, the postcards stopped coming.

My marriage to Eric continued in its off-balance way. I had a miscarriage in late January, and when I went to the doctor for a follow-up appointment, he told me the pregnancy had been more advanced than he had first thought, three months instead of two. Over dinner that evening, I brazenly told Eric what the doctor had said. He simply shrugged and said, "Medicine is sometimes less accurate than we think." Then later, in silence, we sipped wine in the living room. As we rose to go to bed, Eric began to switch off the lights. He voice low, his face completely in shadow, he said, "Despite what you think, Jenny, I have never been unfaithful to you."

"Do you know him?" The proprietress asks again, more firmly the second time.

My tone cautious, my eyes avoiding hers, I say, "I have heard of Hans Sokolov; he may have been a distant acquaintance of my former husband. He is a doctor, I believe."

I look up, then out the window; it is no longer raining. Within moments Jonas walks into the shop, his hair wet; following him is the proprietress's former husband. And I recall the man wearing charcoal-colored pants walking swiftly past me and the woman sitting in a chair with a red stain on her lap.

Five

The Memory

The memory startles, as if you've been doused with an outpouring of water from a sudden rainstorm. Parts are blurry, extended moments completely flooded, too murky to discern. Yet fragments of it are enlarged and clear, revealing images not visible at first.

The recollection comes when least expected, first on a rainy night driving north, passing an accident, then several days later as your gaze fell on the small wooden statue of a Native American woman you purchased soon after your marriage, the first one. You picked it up, held it to the light, but the memory was lost. Have there been suggestions of this incident in the past that were as innocuous as the gentle recollections of your time in Hartford, memories that did not alarm or confuse, that were accepted as part of your childhood, that were not extraordinary?

You close your eyes and try to think back not only to recall the details of the day, but to exist in the time and season. Were there many in the apartment or just a few? Where was the man coming from when he abruptly walked past you? Had he evoked an aura of smothering heat? There were not many rooms in the apartment. Was he older, middle-aged, or younger?

You close your eyes more tightly, hoping to push past the images, to be there. Why were you, a child, dispassionate? Why did you believe this occurrence would always stay with you? Have there been inklings of this memory over the years, suggestions of it, luring you to recall? Have you refused to do so?

Have you focused on your present life alone, not allowing the past to envelop you? Years ago, needing to accept your parents, how different they were, and then your marriage to a man you felt obliged to accept. Had you so much to cope with? Has your marriage to Jonas freed you to recall a painful memory? Is it real or just a compilation of recollections—perhaps not all occurring on the same day?

Yet you deeply believe it happened in the first Hartford apartment, the fragments of it you recall—standing on a rug in the living room, the woman sitting in a chair against the wall, her legs spread open as a man would sit. Your vision of the memory expands—in the corner diagonally across from you, perched on a dusty table, was the small black-and-white television set—but instantaneously your recollection contracts. Where was your mother? Your father? Were you the lone child in the room?

Your frustration grows; something stops you from reliving it, from recalling more. You feel it in the present but can only view it, ponder it from the distance of your current life, only in the past tense.

Such thoughts run through your mind in a matter of seconds.

Six

The Carinis

The memory, the impression it creates, vanishes. Fully in the present, I press my hands to the table and get up to leave; the proprietress watches me closely. Gently, in the manner of a maternal aunt, she touches my wrist, tells me her name is Mara. "Please come again," she says, her head slightly to the side, a flash of anxiety in her eyes. Then she stands; crossing her arms, she nods in the direction of her former husband who, at the counter, impatiently taps his finger against the glass case covering an array of delicate pastries. She leans toward me and I pick up the scent of Chanel. In an emphatic whisper, she says, "I must go to Roberto—Roberto Carini, he likes to say," her inflection a blend of pride and irony.

Jonas, approaching, meets my gaze, then lowers his eyes. I sense he is uneasy. Walking with him to the doorway, I steal a glance at Mara and Roberto. In the presence of her former husband she exudes a combination of the relaxed attitude of people who reside on the Riviera as well as an inherent practicality. Roberto is animated, his cheeks flushed. Hastily he eyes me then looks away. He and Mara speak rapidly in Italian; he is giving her news of some sort. His eyes are hawk-like; hers are fixed on his. Though not touching, their bodies, his more forceful like a bird of prey and hers as deft as a sparrow, are distinctly synchronous.

After the rain, in the emerging sunlight, the pavement glistens. As we walk back to the hotel, Jonas is quiet, meditative, his steps languorous, his lips pursed.

Roberto Carini—there is a sound of familiarity to the name, but too vague, a strain to recall; soon I no longer try. Jonas, pensive, but with an edge to his words, tells me about his time at the museum, the art he finds interesting, especially a Klimt he'd not been familiar with. He is surprised that this small town holds an extensive collection. Then before we reach the incline to the hotel, he stops walking; he turns to me, rests his hands warmly, steadily on each of my arms. With a forced clarity, he says that the man at the café, the one standing at the counter, had asked as they were going into the shop if his family name was

Stram. "How did you answer?" I reflexively ask. He shrugs, replying that he simply ignored the question, pretended he did not hear it. I tell Jonas I find it odd, that maybe someone recognized me. I add that the person who made a scene at the restaurant last night may have been a woman named Isa Sokolov, whom I had met very briefly in New York. I thought she had seemed familiar.

"Have you been to this town before?" he asks.

"No. I have been to the Riviera a few times, but not here."

Jonas studies me, his expression intensely curious. Then suddenly he smiles broadly, with no trace of irony. "You expect a certain amount of anonymity in a small town in another country," he pointedly says as we walk up the incline to the hotel. The sun, now very strong, beats down on us; with each step I feel more and more disoriented, not knowing whether or not to tell him about the other Sokolovs, Hans and Caleb, or about the postcard.

A few days pass before I recall Roberto Carini. Jonas and I are tasting hors d'oeuvres and drinking wine in the lobby. No one else has come down yet this evening. When we speak, there is a slight echo. Though shadows cross the sofas and tables, the sun will not set for a while.

Because of the heat over these past few days, Jonas has put aside sketching. Mostly we have spent our time lounging by the sea beneath an umbrella. The Sokolovs seem distant now, as undefinable as figures in the background of an impressionist painting. As Jonas takes a sip of wine, I notice how his deep tan affirms both his earnestness and his mild sense of irony.

A clacking sound—high heels over marble—deflects my attention. I look up toward the reception desk and recognize the woman I noticed standing alone on the balcony the night of the disturbance at the restaurant. She walks hurriedly toward the exit. She appears to be older than I first thought, maybe in her mid- to late forties, and is quite thin. Her movements suggest she may be late for an engagement. The off-the-shoulder turquoise dress she wears, a straight cut, falls just past her knees. Johanna, my mother, is much more physically solid than this woman, yet is invariably rushing off in a frenzied manner. I recall the turquoise-and-brown dress she hastily stitched for me on her new sewing machine for my thirteenth birthday. Then coming to mind is the turquoise dress she purchased for an occasion she and my father attended in New York. I was sixteen years old and though I did not attend the event, I had driven into the city with them.

But what preceded the trip to New York is what I recall; connecting it to our time spent in the city is like piecing together a mosaic. Though my memory—flashes of various conversations at the time—may not be exact, I am able to imagine from both my recollection of how I would converse with my parents at that age and the information I have learned since coming to the Riviera, what could have occurred, what might have been said.

It would have begun on an afternoon in late fall. Upon catching sight of the invitation I would have been drawn to the swirling dark letters forming the name on the return address: Roberto Carini. Having just returned home from school, I would have noticed the card on the shelf next to the front door. I would have been encouraged—my parents rarely received an invitation. As I picked up the card, I would have felt a deep sense of anticipation, and would have pensively traced the letters of his name with my finger. Delighted for my parents—since their move to Massachusetts they had regarded themselves as outsiders and were rarely invited to an event—I also would have been anxious that they might not attend. I would have felt my mother's presence as she stood behind me looking over my shoulder, a large shadow covering me, protective and at the same time creating a chill.

"I did not know you were home," she said, easily extracting the card from my hand. She wore a brown-and-gray plaid poncho; the fringe on the wide hem grazing my arm as she loosened the invitation from my grasp.

"It's an invitation," I said evenly, meeting her gaze.

She looked deep into my eyes and said, her voice edgy, "Jenny, darling, some invitations are hopeful and social, and I know you want this for your father and me, but this one is not a happy one for us; we will go because you might say we are obliged to attend."

"But you haven't opened it," I insisted, feeling discouraged.

"I don't need to open it, Jenny; it is because of who it is from. He is a rich and impervious entrepreneur from Trieste who has lived for some years in America," she said, placing the invitation back on the shelf. "Attending his event will be a reminder of sad days."

"You don't have to go," I answered, deeply disappointed.

"That is not true, Jenny," she said, opening the door.

I watched as she walked down the front steps, a breeze ruffling her poncho, the outline of her shoulders appearing more erect than usual, her movements more stiff.

Once she had driven away, I picked up the card and went to the large front window; holding the invitation up to the fading afternoon light, I pressed it against the cool glass. Slowly some words became evident. What I determined was that the event would be the first Saturday in January. It would be in New York but I could not make out the name of the hotel. After moving the envelope farther up against the glass, I understood that the event had to do with an opening of an office in Manhattan.

At dinner that night, hearing determination in my voice, I asked my mother if she had read the invitation. My father did not respond; he had always been slow to react as well as adept at hiding his thoughts.

Rising from her seat to go into the kitchen, she said, "I don't need to. I know when and where it is."

"You know everything about it?" I asked, my curiosity piqued.

She nodded, and then I lost sight of her.

"Is Roberto Carini from Trieste?" I called out to her, then looked steadily at my father.

"We only know people from there," he answered with unabashed frankness.

"Roberto Carini is from Trieste," my mother said, coming through the doorway, carrying a large bowl of salad. She tossed back her head and said, "His wife, I believe, is from the Riviera—she had encouraged him to bring the small business he had opened in Italy to the United States." With a sense of finality she placed the bowl on the table. I looked at my parents and noticed how my father gazed down at his salad, his eyeglasses, which he had recently begun to wear on occasion, sliding forward; he intently studied what was before him, his cupped hands resting on the table, on either side of the bowl, as if he were about to attempt an experiment. My mother waited a minute or two before picking up her fork. She looked straight ahead, her posture erect, inhaling and exhaling, her expression softer than usual. Outside the window, it was pitch dark.

What I next recall is accompanying my mother to a shop on Newbury Street to help her choose a dress for the occasion. Impatiently, she tried on each dress the salesman had suggested, then she'd study herself in the three-way mirror, her expression exacting, pensive and highly critical. She intended to look her best but I sensed her uneasiness and doubted she would find the appropriate dress. After an hour or so, she chose a turquoise-colored evening dress that suited her, causing her to look younger. The sleeves of the dress flared at her wrists, and the A-line shape of it softened her form. She was about forty-six at the time. She had studied to become an opera singer and, like most opera singers, the older she became, the less attractive her body; once curvy and voluptuous, it had become dense and strong looking.

When we left the dress shop, she said, "I've done my duty—or I should say almost so." I remember her words and although I was accustomed to my mother's use of language, her syntax, her emphatic and often unexpected way of expressing herself, I was not accustomed to her reining in her nature—she mostly did as she pleased. But this event was different. I was uneasy about it.

About two weeks later, on a warmer than usual day in early December, my mother and I drove into the city to look at the holiday lights on Boston Common. I was slightly melancholic; it struck me that in a few years I would be in college and would not be available to visit the city with her at this time of year. But she was happy that day; she was not frequently cheerful and soon I became caught up in her spirited mood and less guarded about what I said to her. I had always been careful not to use words that would affect my mother's frame of mind. Her mood easily changed and it was pleasant to be with her when she was more optimistic. For she had a dark side to her; she could become brooding, cynical.

After viewing the lights, we stopped to have a cup of tea at a shop across the street. It was growing dark earlier with each passing day. Sitting close to a window framed with silver tinsel, we looked out at the blue-black evening and how the lights shone brightly in contrast, casting a reflection and shadow across my mother's face. She looked content. Her eyes seemed less on guard, more relaxed.

"Who is Roberto Carini?" I asked, eyeing her as I took a sip of tea.

Although she seemed surprised by my question she did not appear suspicious or questioning.

"You are talking about the name on the invitation, aren't you, Jenny dear?"

"Yes, you never do what doesn't please you, and now you feel obligated to go to this event. If you were happy about it I would not be curious; you are uncertain about attending—but you are going."

"It doesn't often happen that you must do something you truly don't want to do," she began. "Usually this occurs only in very sad situations. Yet this event is not in the least meant to be sad."

"Why go, Mother?" I asked, hearing alarm and defiance in my voice.

She leaned forward in her seat and patted my hand with her warm, round one. "Jenny," she said, "Roberto Carini has been good to many people from Trieste. He has helped the community rise and restore itself. And yet he has many sides to him. He is a very successful businessman. In a way it is an honor to have received the invitation. And there will be other people from Trieste at the event; some were very good to us, and so we must go." Her eyes were suddenly melancholic. And I recalled how soon after our move to Massachusetts I had come home early from school and had found her wearing a kimono, haltingly singing what I would later learn is "Vien, diletto, è in ciel la luna," from Bellini's opera *The Puritans*. Crossing her face was the same expression. She now looked out at the darkening evening, her reflection an older and more solemn version of herself. When she turned toward me I saw in her eyes both a sense of pride and one of hurt. I looked down at the table, at the pale pink-and-yellow linen cloth covering it. "Look, Jenny," she said suddenly, her voice hoarse and wistful. "It is snowing."

The only recollections I hold of that weekend are of my mother rendering a detailed and detached description of a woman's dress—perhaps it was Roberto's wife—and my father suggesting we say good-bye to Roberto as we checked out of the hotel. I do not know if they did speak to Roberto that afternoon or whether or not I had been introduced to him. For in memory a curtain has been drawn.

Now I feel Jonas's hand on mine. "Are you okay, Jenny? You seem far away." I nod and study his hopeful eyes and how the lines of his mouth now suggest a subtle irony. Then I reach out and press my finger to his lips, hoping to silence his doubts.

After dinner and a long walk by the sea, we go up into our room. Our bed is covered in a pool of moonlight, beckoning us to submerge ourselves.

The next morning Jonas awakens, sprawled on his back with his arms outstretched. His forehead is hot and moist. A summer flu, I think. He looks at me, he appears pale and weary. Soon he drifts off. Once I am assured he is sleeping I open the sliding glass door and go out onto the balcony.

The day is sunny, with no breeze. But there is a haze in the sky muting the bright light. The ocean is calm and mellow this morning. Below and off to the side I see part of the pool. From what I can determine no one is in it; I do not hear splashing or voices.

I think of my conversation with Mara and long to go back and speak with her, hear more of her story. I wonder what she knows of Hans or maybe even Caleb. Again, the memory of the woman with a red stain on her lap and the man with the charcoal-colored pants comes to mind. And I am more distraught by it than before.

* * *

While Jonas sleeps I take the elevator down to the outdoor restaurant near the pool for a late breakfast. I see the French family at the table next to mine. The husband picks up the child from his seat, then holds him in his lap and feeds him with his fork. Aware I am sitting not far from her, Helen turns to me. She's wearing a white floppy hat and dark glasses. I cannot see her eyes. "Your husband, is he away?" Her strong French accent is disarming.

"He might have a flu, but I am certain he will be better if not tomorrow, then in the next few days," I say. Reflexively, I ask about the woman at her table, some nights ago, was she not well?

"That is my aunt," she answers and sighs. "Sometimes she is well and sometimes she is not. She is in Tuscany now and will spend the remainder of the summer there. Her husband owns this hotel. They live in a beautiful home down the road," she says, pointing in no particular direction. Her lips are thin; she smiles slightly. "She is my mother's sister; both were born in Trieste. Their parents separated before the war. My mother went with their mother to France. And my aunt went to America with their father." She shrugs, and before turning away, she adds, "My father, of course, is French."

I bring Jonas a cup of hot tea. I sit close to him; he drinks from the cup. He is only able to take a few sips, then drops his head back onto the pillow. Once he is asleep, I go out to the balcony. I will wait until he is better before going into town and speaking again with Mara.

His voice weak, Jonas calls out for me. Leaving the balcony door open, I go back into the room. But I realize he is asleep; he is dreaming. I lean close to him. "Stram," he says clearly, then he mumbles nonsensical syllables, turning his body slightly to the left and then to the right. His expression is pained. I wait. Soon he is still and sleeping, his demeanor now calm.

Out on the balcony, I hear the sound of the waves, the clattering of the dishes below, the waiters clearing up the breakfast plates and cups. From the bedroom comes Jonas's breathing, alternately even then staggered. In the lounge chair, I close my eyes and drift off to sleep. In my dream Eric and I are out on a patio, overlooking the sea, but we are not on the Riviera. The environment is not as restful as the Mediterranean. Uncertain where we are, I am uneasy; fearful of the answer, I do not ask him. There is a strong, cool breeze. Maybe it is Bar Harbor in early fall, or south Florida on a cool day in January. Certainly it is the Atlantic Ocean; it is because of the dampness, the harshness of the breaking waves, the chill in the air that I have never felt on the Mediterranean. Eric wears dark glasses. I lean forward, attempt to read the expression in his eyes, hoping to comprehend his mood; I cannot penetrate his thoughts, who he is. I press him with questions and he doesn't respond. The pain caused by his silence is unbearable. When I open my eyes, the Mediterranean is before me, the warm air caressing—I have escaped my dream. Yet I recall the last time I was with Eric. We were driving to the airport. It was a cool day in November, and the air was damp. "You are sick, Eric. You shouldn't be going."

"It's business," he answered.

"You mean the business you help someone else run."

"I can't disappoint him, Jenny."

"If he were as nice as you say, he would understand you are too sick to go to Key West."

He looked over at me and smiled. "You'd like him, I should introduce you."

"It is surprising, Eric, that you have not done so. I don't even know his name, only that you refer to him as Il Capo."

I do not recall what I last said to him, I can't remember him leaving the car. Did we lightly kiss good-bye? I have no recollection of our parting and do not believe I went into the airport with him. What I do remember is parking the car in front of the terminal, and Eric gingerly running his fingers through my hair, and lightly touching my face, my neck as if for the first time. Then he was no longer with me.

Looking out at the Mediterranean and then over to the side, I spot Roberto Carini in his bathing trunks facing the pool, his arms crossed—fourteen years ago my mother and father attended an event hosted by him. I imagine that was where they reconnected with Eric and his parents after some years. People I have not seen since we lived in Hartford will be there, most from Trieste, my mother had said, her eyes sorrowful. Yes, Trieste, where she had studied opera. I think again of that day I had come upon her wearing a white-and-red kimono, her arms extended, her voice hesitant, wistful, as she sang from the score of *The Puritans*.

Seven

The Cousins

Not until Jonas has fully recovered and is sketching with his usual intensity will I realize what should have been obvious. It will dawn on me as if, sitting in a dark theater, I am startled by a flood of lights at the conclusion of the movie. After the effect of sudden illumination subsides, in silence and from within, I experience my vulnerability, my loss, a dimming of insight.

On the beach on a Friday afternoon, I have neglected to bring my dark glasses, and the sun is blinding. A trace of a breeze carries with it the prickly smell of salt and sea. The sand is hot and loose. Next to me is the French woman, Helen. While Jonas was recovering from the flu, in a casual way we became friendly.

A short distance away, Jonas is perched on a small hill of rocks overlooking the Mediterranean; a piece of charcoal in his grasp, he moves his hand across the art pad, a sudden and abbreviated wind ruffles the short sleeves of his T-shirt. It is gratifying to see him healthy and involved in his work again. At the water's edge, Helen's husband Marc plays with their son Remy. As a wave breaks against the rocky shore, he lifts the boy with his sturdy hands. Above the swirling water, the child moves his feet as if bicycling, the dark wet sand and a scattering of pebbles cling to his feet. Marc seems more of a maternal figure than Helen; though I like her, her directness, her honesty.

The more I speak with Helen, the more I glean how different she is from Isa. Whenever she raises her head from what she's been reading, she'll slide her sunglasses to the end of her nose and I'll note again and again how her eyes are the same shape and dark brown like Isa's, but her forehead is narrower and her chin round instead of pointy like her aunt's. There is a frankness in her gaze unlike the impetuous avoidance I found in her aunt's eyes, as if Isa lacked a center, an identity. But I was younger then and wasn't seeking wholeness.

Now Helen closes the book and leans her head back against her lounge chair, her wide-brimmed hat casting a shadow across the side of her face. She tells me that she and Marc are deciding whether or not to have another child—she is inclined not to, but she isn't certain if she wants Remy not to have a brother or a sister. She doesn't want him to be alone; yet she is still not convinced. "What about you, Jenny? You and Jonas have no children?" With her index finger she pushes up her sunglasses; I no longer see her eyes. She is providing me with a sense of privacy and perhaps an option not to respond. Yet she does not open her book. Glancing at the cover, I see it is by the French writer, Céline. With only a vague knowledge of the author and a sparse understanding of French, I translate the title as *Journey to the End of the Night*. She gazes away, in the direction of her son and husband, a breeze flapping up the towel at the foot of her chair.

I explain that Jonas is my second husband, and then briefly describe my uneven marriage to Eric, his death, how he had been most likely swept off or had fallen from a yacht in Key West. He'd had a severe flu and had been taking a good deal of medicine. He was disoriented. I pause, wait for her to absorb what I have told her, then add that I have not yet considered having a child. Jonas and I have discussed it only in passing, in theory, never with intent, I say. I tell her that I miscarried during my first marriage.

Helen lowers her glasses, turns toward me, smiling kindly. "I am sorry about your miscarriage," she responds thoughtfully. She is quiet for a moment, then says, "You are young to have been married twice. It is very sad to hear of your first husband's tragic death. You say you were not compatible; because of this it must have been devastating for you."

There is something in her openness, her warmth, the expression in her discerning gaze, that is familiar. But I recall the eyes as blue, not brown like Helen's, and it now strikes me that she and Caleb are cousins. Startled, I draw away, from my initial perception of her, and study Helen closely. She returns my look as straightforwardly as Caleb would have. Thoughts of Caleb, his earnestness, his quick, strong energy evoke distant memories of pain and joy.

"What is it, Jenny?" Helen asks. "Have I upset you? I should not have spoken to you in a familiar way?"

"No, Helen, not at all. Eric's passing is very tragic and painful, and I think more so, as you say, because we did not get along."

"But you are fortunate to know Jonas. He is, I believe, not superficial and very loyal." She smiles encouragingly.

"Yes, I have known him for a long time, since I was eighteen. He was at first my neighbor, later my friend," I say, feeling a sense of dislocation, and ask her if she has any siblings.

"Yes, two sisters, one older, one younger—you see, I am the middle child. My mother's sister had only one child, and we would visit America once a year and my aunt and her family would come to France once a year. And so we knew our cousin. But he was an only child and I always thought he seemed lonely. Yet you are an only child, didn't you say, Jenny, and so is your husband? Or was it Jonas who told me? You do not seem lonely, nor does your husband, but I guess that is my assumption."

"I have never felt lonely. My mother had two miscarriages, I've been told, one in Trieste and one when she lived in Connecticut. Your mother was born in Trieste too, you said the other day. I wonder if they know of each other."

"So many coincidences," Helen says, appearing puzzled.

"It is not really surprising," I answer. Then I tell her how a few months ago I discovered the postcard my first husband, had sent, with the hotel on the front. "It is not unusual I would meet people from Trieste here; your aunt's husband is from Trieste and so was Eric."

Her voice sensitive, she asks what Eric was like. I feel a sense of panic; I was never quite sure. "Eric was much older than me—twenty years, in fact—and as I said he too was born in Trieste. His parents helped mine during the war, shielded them as my father was a member of an anti-fascist group. And during all the turbulence of that time, my mother had desperately longed to become an opera singer. Eric was a young boy during the war; naturally it was traumatic for him."

"What was his family name?"

"Stram. I believe they were well known in the city, but came to the United States after the war, returning to Trieste before Eric and I married. I felt obliged to marry him in a way. But it was my decision to do so. I was overwhelmed by him, by the attention he gave me, and I thought I was more mature than I was. I was under an illusion." I hear my voice sounding factual and distant, shielding my emotions which are swirling, muddling my recollections of my marriage to Eric and my affair with Caleb.

"Stram—the name is familiar, but I can't quite place it," she says. I see she is somewhat uneasy.

Her husband is coming up from the shore, their son Remy walking beside him, holding his hand, tugging at it, wanting to go back to the sea. Marc looks down at the little boy, who is jumping up and down, kicking sand; soon they are going toward the small café behind us. Helen nods at them and smiles as they pass us. She says something very quickly in French to them.

Now as she turns to me I say, "You mentioned your aunt is in Tuscany. Will you see her again before you go back to France?"

"Yes, Aunt Isa will be mostly alone until the end of the month; her husband needs to remain on the Riviera because of his business interests. He is not completely retired. He has meetings at the hotel with partners of his, but he will go in early September to join my aunt. We will travel to Tuscany to see her after we leave here in a week; her son will be visiting her, as well as my two sisters and their families and my mother. My father is too busy with his work, he says, but he has never been fond of my aunt. We will have a reunion weekend of sorts. Her first husband may come too; they still communicate. He may come with her son."

As Helen speaks in her matter-of-fact and unerringly honest way, I am startled—though she does not speak their names—by her innocent reference to Hans and Caleb. I lower my head to avoid her gaze. Hearing her mention them in this way is disquieting—for naturally she does not realize my past intimacy with her cousin and my knowledge of Hans and Isa. Yet what I find most disconcerting is that my connection to them is severed; they are strangers.

On the table next to her chair I notice Orwell's novel *1984*. "You read in English, too, Helen?"

"Yes, I am a translator, you see. I think it will be good to read this book as it is the same year as now."

"Our lives are not like that at all," I counter. "There is no big brother watching over us."

"Yes, but it could occur at another time, maybe not too far away," she says in an even and thoughtful way.

Helen lowers her head and begins to read again from the Céline novel, and I lie back in the chaise longue. After a while I look over at her; she grasps the book in two hands, her expression focused as if she is deriving something essential from it, as if she is being fed by the contents of the book. I recall how in the past my mother would often say that serious novelists from Europe touch your soul. Americans do not want their souls to be touched, I have concluded; they want them to be free, uncluttered.

In the distance I see Jonas waving at me and guess he wants me to come and look at his sketches. Walking toward him, I feel the heat from the sand through my thin sandals. I remove my shoes, then climb up the warm hill of rocks. Once I reach him, he turns his pad over and places a stone on it. He moves close and puts his arm around me. I look out at the beauty of the Mediterranean; it is as if we are miles from the shore, the beach a good distance away. I feel a fine breeze and the pressure of Jonas's arm across my shoulders. When I look over at him, his eyes avert from my gaze. "Jenny," he begins, and I look straight ahead, feeling a stab of anxiety within.

Up ahead, a few yards from us, I catch sight of the British couple swimming in the sea. I have not seen them since that rainy day at the tourist office in the town center, asking about different beaches in the area. I am surprised they are here. They are frolicking, splashing water at each other.

I look over at Jonas; his expression reveals frustration more than anger. "What are you thinking?" I ask, urging him to speak.

"Why would that man have asked if my name was Stram? Do you know him, Jenny?"

"I had no recollection of him when we came to the hotel," I say, my words muffled by the overwhelming strength of the sun. "But I remembered him soon after his name was mentioned by his former wife; she is the one who is the proprietress at the café. Her name is Mara, and his is Roberto Carini. He purchased the shop for her after their divorce." And I fill in the details about the event in New York my parents attended long ago and how I had not heard his name again until Mara spoke of him that day in the café. I add that he may have been the business mogul Eric had worked for. He might have been the one who had instructed Eric to go to Key West—maybe he did not know how poorly Eric had been feeling, but for some reason Eric could not refuse his request. Then I tell Jonas that Roberto Carini owns the hotel we are staying in.

"Stram," he says, "maybe in some convoluted way he associates us with Eric." He smiles. "But it isn't so convoluted, is it, Jenny?"

Warily, I smile at his humor, a blend of warmth and dry sarcasm.

As I walk over the hot sand back to the lounge chair, the grains sieving into my sandals, burning my heels, the memory strikes me again. It is in a different way this time. What comes to mind is not the woman, but the man, his feet, how narrow they were, so narrow for his size. But then I am shaken out of it by the sight of Helen bent over her book, and again I see her resemblance to Caleb.

I lie down in the lounge chair and close my eyes, feel the piercing rays on my eyelids. As I inhale the sea air, I hear the waves breaking and the water sloshing onto the shore. When I open my eyes and look over at Helen, I see she has stopped reading and is looking away. She is not bothered by the heat; it energizes her. She turns to look over at her son and husband who are now in the chair next to her. Remy has fallen asleep across his father's stomach.

I look out at Jonas on the rocks, wondering if he wants to go inside, if the sun is too strong now, but he seems to be sketching more intently than before. And I feel a sense of anticipation, the heavy sand, the intensity of the sun, and the sound of the sea, mostly soothing, but thunderous whenever a huge wave hits the shore.

Soon I hear Helen's voice, crinkly now, "Jenny, it is a lovely day, isn't it? Your husband relishes it—look at how he sketches, with joy."

I gaze in the distance at Jonas and smile.

"It is too bad we will be leaving in a week," she says, her voice pensive.

"Your family reunion in Tuscany is something you might enjoy, though; Tuscany is beautiful too."

"Yes, it is true. But I do not know how relaxing it will be. I am concerned about my aunt. When I think of her behavior that night, I realize she has never been this unwell. My mother will be upset by her condition. Both her former husband and son are doctors; they have a better understanding of why she is this way. She is erratic. Roberto's approach to Isa is practical. He only stays with her when she is well; when she isn't, he sends her to their home in Tuscany and he goes off to speak to his ex-wife—if she isn't working at her café, then he'll take a short flight and visit her at her Paris apartment. I don't know her well; her name is Mara, but she is the reason my aunt and her husband divorced. They had an affair—Aunt Isa's first husband and Mara. Isa couldn't forgive him. It was good Roberto was there to support Aunt Isa at the time—they comforted each other." Listening to her, I conclude her words about Mara are not fully accurate; she has been exposed only to Isa's point of view. There is more, I surmise.

An echoing distant scream interrupts our talk. Helen and I look toward the sea; in water up to her neck, the English woman is waving her arms, crying out for help.

Eight

The Lovers

"They are lovers," Helen tells us, her voice hushed, then she lowers her eyes as if troubled by her words. It is twilight; she and Marc, Jonas and I are out on the patio, sipping wine. Our dinner plates have been cleared away. During the meal, we refrained from talking about the incident, which, I believe, struck us at different moments, as if in concert with the rotating light surrounding the pool, spotting the back of the hotel, then the water in the pool, the flattened stone floor of the patio, and lastly and individually, each of us at the table.

Quiet and awed by the near drowning and rescue we witnessed only hours before, we look away as she speaks;

Marc fixedly stares up at the hotel, toward the room, where Remy sleeps; his sitter is a sixteen-year-old girl from the town. Jonas's eyes wander in the direction of the ocean, not far away, and I gaze across the pool and watch the pianist behind the glass doors, his shoulders gracefully rising and falling, his music barely audible. Helen's straw hat is on the table next to her glass; with one finger she taps the brim where there is a slight tear; her motion is lulling, like the now-muted sound of the ocean.

From a distance, it seems, Jonas asks, "Aren't we all?" I turn, expecting to see irony in his eyes, but instead his gaze is direct; he studies each of us.

Helen explains what she means is that they are married, but not to each other. While she speaks an image flashes across my mind: Jonas diving off the hill of rocks and swimming rapidly toward the woman, his swift, surreal strokes, the sun burnishing the red color of her hair, her desperate cries for help. At first I was filled with pride and hope, but soon I felt a sense of devastation, remembering Eric's death. And the frenzied motion of Jonas's arms awakened the memory of the man in charcoal-gray pants walking quickly by. Then, almost instantaneously, I was freed by the sight of the lifeguard in a small boat motoring out to save her and the man I had believed was her husband, rescuing the couple before Jonas reached them.

"You were brave, Jonas," Helen says, looking over at him, her expression sincere.

"Not really—I don't think I would have reached them in time."

Marc, who is more inclined to listen than speak, says, "You were brave, Jonas; it was your instinct, your humanity that compelled you to save them. You are not like the average person, you are better, *auguste*—in English, 'august,' what you call this month. You would do the same again, I think. For you, it is natural."

Jonas, not accustomed to flattery, looks away, toward the ocean; his expression tightening, his face appearing more angular now. I interject, "You are very kind, but I believe either of you would have done the same."

"Yes, I agree," Jonas says, facing us now. "If you were perched where I was, most anyone would have done the same."

"But I am a poor swimmer," Helen says, emphatically. With one swift movement she thrusts the hat on top of her head, as if covering her ineptitude.

Marc responds, "Though I am an adequate swimmer, I do not know if I would have had Jonas's instinct. I would have been fearful of not possessing the strength to bring them in." He looks over at me and asks, "Jenny, can you swim?"

"Only moderately well, not well enough to rescue anyone, unfortunately. I do not know if I would have jumped in as reflexively as Jonas. On second thought, it does take a certain type of person to extend him or herself in such a way, a selfless person, I think." I ramble on, but when I look around the table I see the others are focusing on my words. And so I change the subject. Looking at Helen, I ask, "How do you know they are married to other people?"

Carefully she removes her hat and places it on the table. "My aunt Isa's husband Roberto told me. He isn't certain if the man will survive—he has been hospitalized—but the woman will be fine. She was crying out to save him; apparently she is a better swimmer than he is."

As Helen speaks in her precise and honest way, relaying only the facts she is aware of, not wanting to pass judgment, she again taps the brim of her hat with her finger. But suddenly she looks up, and I follow her gaze. Roberto is approaching our table, his walk slow and purposeful. I feel a sense of anxiety, attempting to imagine him as a younger man, how he and Eric might have interacted. Eric would have been respectful, would have deferred to what I surmised would have been Roberto's instructions, his exacting demands.

"Any news, Roberto?" Helen asks in English.

"The woman is on a plane back to London, and the man's wife has arrived and is on her way to the hospital. His condition is very serious."

After he finishes speaking, he sits down in the empty seat and crosses his legs; his gaze fixed on me, he says in a direct voice, "You are Eric Stram's widow. My wife, who is now in Tuscany, recognized you; she said she met you once."

Reflectively I introduce Jonas as my husband.

Roberto nods at Jonas but does not extend his hand.

"Your parents," Roberto asks, "are they well?"

"Yes," I say, wondering if I met him that weekend in New York years ago.

Helen looks at me, her expression startled, and says, "I did not realize you had met my aunt Isa."

"It was a quick meeting, and the night I noticed her at dinner, I wasn't certain if she was the same woman I had met in New York."

Helen doesn't say anything but a puzzled expression crosses her face. She turns to her uncle and asks again about the couple. But Roberto doesn't respond, apparently wanting to move on, past that situation, on to another topic. He looks over again at me, meeting my gaze. His eyes are a steel gray color, framed by his bushy brows, his skin is a dark olive and his stare is sharp and inquisitive, experienced, and I feel a sense of familiarity. Jonas clasps my hand, resting on my lap.

Roberto raises his finger, not in a hostile way, but warmly, as if he knows me. A half smile crossing his lips, he says, "Eric Stram, I first knew him as a young boy in Trieste. He was quiet, shy. He didn't speak for a few years. People thought it was because of the war. It was a mystery. Why did young Eric Stram stop talking? It would have been more of a mystery if it hadn't been for the war, but from time to time people did wonder. His mother Alma is a woman who is both intelligent and beautiful in that you ask yourself if she is more intelligent than beautiful, or vice versa."

"Can't a woman or man be both?" Helen chimes in, and we all laugh.

Roberto calls over the waiter, ordering everyone another round of drinks. We neither decline nor accept his offer. When the wine comes, we sit and drink as if to still our nerves, not knowing what he will say next. For Roberto's presence is commanding, not easy to escape.

By the time he speaks further, it is dark, the rotating light around the pool brighter now in contrast. The ocean appears more distant; it is nearly impossible to discern the steady rise and fall of the waves.

After a long silence, Roberto says, "I was partial to little Eric. Maybe he was shy because his parents were so well-known in Trieste. His father was a wealthy banker and his mother was involved in volunteer work. She would go to the homes of those who were most ill and read to them. His parents took in yours, Mrs. Stram; your father was solidly against fascism, was rumored to have taken part in actions against the government. He needed to be protected and the Strams took it upon themselves to do so. Eric's older brother had died before the war in an unfortunate accident—I can't remember the details but it was because of a childish act on the part of one of his friends. It was more tragic because of the idiocy of it all."

Roberto crosses his legs, leans back in his chair, and closes his eyes. I wonder if he has fallen asleep. I grasp the narrow arms of my chair and begin to rise, ready now to leave. I am filled with anguish, remembering only Eric's death, not his life. But Jonas touches my wrist to stop me, and I sit down; he whispers in my ear, "It is better to stay, to listen, he may say more."

I look over at Helen and then Marc, across the table from each other; they seem quite still, half-intoxicated, half under the spell of Roberto. Marc winks nervously at Helen; she tightly closes her eyes, suddenly opening them as if startled. The reflection of the rotating light surrounding the pool crosses her face and I see another side of Helen, one more like Isa, a stark and stoic expression, but once the light passes, she again seems her straightforward self.

Roberto, his eyes now open, studies us one by one, nodding as he does so, as if reading a book he is in accord with. Marc sits directly to his left, his narrow shoulders hunched slightly forward, his pointy face, his even expression. Then next to him is Jonas, sitting back in his chair, his expression a complex mix of irony and aspiration, his hands loosely clasping the narrow arms of the chair, very much in the present as well as thinking about other things that may cross his mind, how the ocean is barely visible, how the rotating light strikes the hotel. And when Roberto looks over at me I sense he is thinking not of me, but only of Eric, not Eric the man, but Eric the boy, who was unable to speak, the mysterious Eric, who Roberto eventually took under his hawkish wing. Lastly his gaze meets Helen's; she is to my left, his right, the niece of his second wife. I wonder if he is disillusioned by his second marriage, if he wishes he and Mara had not divorced, and I remember how Helen told me earlier in the day of Mara and Hans's affair. I think of my affair with Caleb, something that isn't real to me; yet the events of this day are hazy as well.

Roberto continues, "Most will never know for certain why young Eric did not speak—was he traumatized by the war or was it something else, another reason? I needed to understand his silence. After his parents moved to America, I invited him to join my business. He was in college at the time. Eric had an uncanny ability to recall people, their faces and names, and so he was good for my business. Clients were relaxed with him, not because he was particularly warm and inviting, but because he remembered who they were."

Surprisingly I hear Helen's voice, as muted as the sound of the lapping waves, asking Roberto, "Did you ever discover why Eric did not speak?" Her words are slurred, as if she has had too much wine. Then she turns to me and says, "Maybe you know, Jenny, maybe you know," but though I hear in her words a yearning for truth, I wonder how much she is aware of what she is saying. It is as if she is speaking in her sleep.

Before I have a chance to respond, Roberto interjects, sounding baffled, which seems antithetical to his nature, "How would Mrs. Stram know? She wasn't in Trieste at the time; it was before her parents came to America, where she was born. No, she does not know why, and may not know that Eric did not speak during the war."

"No, I did not know," I say. "He was not very forthcoming; his tendency was to hide things. He did not like to talk about himself. I always thought he regarded himself as ordinary."

"But he had an uncanny memory for faces and names," Roberto says, shaking his head. "Eric was not ordinary."

"Yes," I say. "It was as if he knew certain people well, people who seemed not to recognize him, as if they were celebrities who naturally do not know their admiring fans." And I think of Isa and Hans Sokolov and how their names had come so easily to Eric's lips even though Isa may not have recalled him at the time, perhaps did not know of him until she married Roberto. But I glean how with Isa things are not as they seem—even her loyal niece has acknowledged her erratic behavior.

"Eric was important to my business because of his reticence as well. His growth—emotional, I guess you could say—was stunted because of his experiences as a young boy. It isn't surprising he married a much younger woman," he says musingly.

I think of the anguish Eric caused during our marriage, the uncertainty I experienced, and I am pained and angry with Roberto's presentation of my former husband as innocent and naïve, perhaps exceptional. Needing to leave,

I look over at Jonas. Just as we stand, Helen says, her voice pensive and dazed, "What possibly could have happened to young Eric?" Jonas takes my hand and we nod good-bye to those round the table, who are enclosed now in near darkness. We walk toward the hotel, and as Jonas opens the door to let us inside, I vaguely hear Roberto's voice, his words like scattered, floating notes from a saxophone being played in the distance—rumors . . . rape . . .

Nine

The Proprietress

"He survived. His wife arrived yesterday evening—he is weak—and the woman, the other one, has returned to London, to her husband, I imagine," Mara says, leaning forward in her seat. There's a seductive note in her tone; an indistinct marbly look in her gaze. She has interrupted our conversation with these words, which have nothing to do with what we've been discussing; they are as dissonant as if, having been immersed in a discussion of impressionism, she deviates to politics.

"You are speaking of the couple at the hotel who nearly drowned. Roberto told you?" She eyes me and nods, the late morning light flows through the open front of the café grazing her red-brown hair and narrow shoulders.

She takes a sip of cappuccino, an unlit cigarette dangling between her fingers. She appears more subdued today.

Awakening early from a hazy dream of Roberto and Mara entwined like branches of a century-old banyan, I felt compelled to speak with her this day.

Over breakfast, I told Jonas that I needed to walk to the town center to buy some incidentals at the pharmacy. He was motioning for the waiter, who immediately came to our table. After ordering more hot coffee and steamed milk, Jonas looked at me, nodded and smiled loosely. Jonas speaks less and less—no more in-depth discussions about line and shadow in Picasso's *Blue Nude* or *The Old Guitarist*. Though he does not talk of it, I gather Jonas is focused on his own work, what he is producing.

Thirty minutes ago I walked into Mara's shop and ordered a cappuccino at the counter; she seemed to vaguely recognize me. I realized she may be accustomed to speaking with customers in an open-ended and confidential way; I was no different from the others. As she prepared my drink, I told her I was in the cafe ten days before and mentioned our conversation about the Sokolovs. Nodding, she did not respond. I sat at a table close by, and four or five children, escorted by two women, came in to the café, asking for gelatos. With a distracted smile Mara served the children. Once they left, she approached my table.

Our conversation began awkwardly. It was more on my part than hers; Italians, particularly those I've observed on the Riviera, do not possess a sense of hesitancy. I gleaned from the time she had served the children and had come to join me, she had mostly recalled our previous conversation, but soon I understood it was more because of what her ex-husband had told her.

Placing her cup on the table, her expression thoughtful, she said that Roberto had noticed me as he was leaving the café the last time I was there, and that I was Jenny Stram, Eric's wife. Mara's speech was more circumspect than I recalled; she seemed to be piecing together our last conversation with Roberto's words.

My pulse quickening, I asked, "You knew Eric?" How familiar of a presence he is here, how uncanny, I thought. But apparently he was a different Eric at the time than I had known, a docile Eric, more aware of others, and even more magnanimous, perhaps.

"Of course I knew Eric," she said, her eyes concerned. "I was married to Roberto for many years—how could I not know Eric? His death was a tragedy for us all. Roberto respected Eric. He knew him as a young boy in Trieste. Although he was not part of Eric's family's milieu—Roberto was quite poor—he would notice young Eric enjoying a cookie at the pastry shop, accompanied by the woman who took care of him. Roberto has always had a good understanding of people; it is why he was very successful in business." She turned her head while speaking to see, it seemed, if there was anyone in hearing distance; except for the two of us, the shop was empty.

She then explained in a staccato-like way, her English less fluid, her Italian inflection more obvious than it was the last time we spoke. Her expression was more contemplative, less wistful. She said that most people in Trieste knew of Eric's family, the Strams. But Roberto was perceptive; he understood that Eric was unlike his family. She continued, saying that on occasion Roberto would deliver packages to the homes of the wealthy, and from time to time he would go to Eric's home. Roberto had known that Eric's older brother had died in an unfortunate accident and, though his parents had been stoic, he thought Eric carried this sadness with him. One day when he brought a package to the Strams—it was before the start of the war—Eric opened the door and whispered something to Roberto, but Roberto could not hear his words. When the maid came to the door Eric ran away. "Of course this is what Roberto told me, how he remembers it," Mara said confidently.

"How old was Eric at the time?" I asked, attempting to organize in my mind the events of my previous husband's life. My heart beat rapidly, I clasped my hands together nervously. Mara eyed my discomfort.

"Roberto must have been in his mid-twenties," she said offhandedly—"Eric may have been five or six."

And it is now that she leans forward and speaks about the man and woman who nearly drowned yesterday afternoon. After asking if Roberto had told her, I add, "My husband and I were on the beach at the time. It is good to know he has survived."

Yet she continues to speak about the couple, deftly diverting me from my intense curiosity about the young Eric.

"Of course Roberto was concerned for their safety, but if either of them had been seriously harmed, it would have severely hurt the reputation of the hotel—it is what Roberto is most proud of."

Finished with her cappuccino, Mara leans back in the chair and lights her cigarette. She alertly eyes the entrance. My back is to the front of the café, but I know by her satisfied and relaxed expression that no one is coming in.

"I first met Eric when he was twenty years old," Mara begins, her gaze distant, focused. "It was in America. Roberto and I lived in Philadelphia at the time. It was before his business became successful. When Roberto discovered through a mutual friend that Eric's family had moved to the United States and that he was attending college in Philadelphia, he called him and invited him to dinner at our home."

As she speaks, I grow more and more apprehensive, fearful of my memory of Eric; it is only a silhouette of him, but it is more intrusive, more daunting than ever was his presence.

Relaxing more in her seat, Mara continues, describes how Eric appeared startled, those blue-gray eyes of his, uncertain as he came into their home awkwardly holding a bouquet of flowers, each one wilting. Promptly she took them from him, buried her face in the bouquet, inhaling, then reached out, touching his shoulder, assuring him how lovely they were. Intuitively she understood how important Eric was to Roberto. She also felt sorry for Eric, how confused he seemed. He was hesitant in this environment, this new country, she gathered. As she speaks, I picture her with Eric: Mara smaller, more confident. Eric, wanting to please her, would have tried to appear less, so she could seem more. Then Mara adds that naturally Eric reminded her husband of those years in Trieste, before the war. To Roberto, although he was quite poor, those were idyllic times. Money wasn't important to him. The simple life was rich and plentiful, the beauty of dawn, the sound of children playing in the large square, the Adriatic, the quietude of the evening hours. Mara extends her arms as she speaks.

Then she lowers her voice and leans forward, "After Eric left our home that night, Roberto said that during the war there had been rumors that the Strams were protecting a couple, the husband, Henri Smila, an anti-fascist, had taken part in precarious activities, the Smilas, your parents. Your father was very brave, Jenny. We may have visited once when your parents lived in Hartford and Roberto and I had a home in Philadelphia but I am not certain—it was years ago."

Upon hearing her words, my heart pounds.

She continues, "This rumor added to Roberto's curiosity about the Strams; he had assumed they were not people who would have involved themselves in a perilous situation—they were not brave or fearless, he had believed, and so at first he discounted the rumor, but later he discovered it to be true.

"The night Eric visited, Roberto questioned him lightly about college—he was, I believe, in his first year—and then spoke to him of his business, how it had started slowly on the Riviera and now in America he wanted it to grow more; his dream was that it would expand throughout the world. He was hoping to draw Eric out of himself."

She says that Eric had not communicated much about school; he had given basically yes and no answers but seemed intrigued when Roberto spoke of his work. Eric's interest had spurred Roberto to describe how he had conceived of his business and in what direction he wanted to take it; as he spoke it struck him that maybe he should hire Eric to work for him—maybe he would discover more about this inscrutable young man.

Roberto soon forgot about the child Eric, as the nearly twenty-year-old Eric had taken to the business adroitly. He left college within the year. Roberto became friendly with Eric's family and the families the Strams were acquainted with in Trieste. They all admired Roberto because Roberto was successful. His financial holdings had grown significantly while theirs had dwindled.

Roberto sent Eric around the world to speak with potential clients. Eric remembered people well, and never revealed too much; he had a natural discipline with words. Roberto trusted his impression of people; Eric was accurate in the way he naturally understood clients, how to assess their interests, their needs. Roberto's business grew, and he always attributed it in part to Eric.

Eventually, Mara says, Roberto opened an office in New York as well, but they continued to live mostly in Philadelphia. After twenty years in America, she and

Roberto returned to Italy, mostly living on the Riviera. Roberto did not see Eric as much as before, though they spoke often on the telephone. And they spent some time together during meetings at the hotel, maybe once or twice a year.

"We did not attend your wedding," Mara adds. "An emergency had come up with one of Roberto's interests in Hong Kong; we happened to be there at the time and could not leave." She pauses, then says, "Roberto did not attend Eric's funeral—it would have been too painful for him, and he did not tell me of your first husband's passing until a month later." Inhaling from her cigarette, she tosses back her head and continues, "It is not surprising Eric never mentioned Roberto to you. I think your former husband may have desired to appear more independent than he actually was. And you were young, most likely not curious about the details of Eric's work, more interested in your own career, I imagine." She sighs. "At that time Roberto wondered less and less about the young Eric. But now with your appearance, Roberto seems intrigued again; it brings back memories to him. Now that he is mostly retired, he has more time to reflect."

"And he shares his thoughts, his concerns with you," I say, and feel myself smiling, thinking how, as confident as her words sound, I do not know if they are entirely true; I understand how foggy memory can be.

"Yes, it is as if we are still married. I blamed myself for the failure of our marriage. I had slipped into an affair with Hans Sokolov, the man we spoke of the last time you were here. We were both unhappy in our marriages. Roberto was very irascible at the time, preoccupied with his business, and Hans's wife, Isa, a flighty personality, appeared not to be interested in her husband any longer. But eventually, I realized Isa had needed us to become involved. She understood we were lonely and flawed, but Hans was less flawed than me. And though I must admit I made the decision as an adult, to go forward with the affair, I wonder how much free will I was exerting—or was it the will of Isa and perhaps even Roberto? I know I sound weak because I was weak to have allowed myself to succumb to Isa's will. If I hadn't, I believe I would not have become involved with Hans and would still be married to Roberto."

My relationship with Caleb comes to mind. "Does anyone ever have free will?" I ask. I think of the memory that has become a shadow I live with every day, no longer startling and unexpected but more and more a part of my life. The child is still alive within me, the young girl who watched dispassionately as a man with charcoal-colored pants rushed by while a woman sat in a chair, a red stain covering her lap.

"I do not know, Jenny. You are young, life must seem very straightforward to you, I imagine. Yet there is something about you; I think you may have had a lover while you were married to Eric. He was much older than you and was often away because of Roberto's business." She lowers her gaze. When she raises her head, she looks past me; her eyes startled, her posture more erect. I turn round; standing in the entrance way, the rays from the noon sun outlining his form, is a slightly older Hans Sokolov. His gaze rests on Mara, and I recall him looking upon his son in the same way, seven years ago, as Caleb walked down the steps of the public library.

Ten

The Letter

All the doors are propped open, and the soft morning air flows through the foyer. Coming in from an early walk, I stop at the front desk. *Un momento, prego*, the clerk says and turns away. Smiling, he then hands me a letter along with the key to my room. It is disconcerting to see Helen's name on the return address; I was not expecting her to write until she returned to Paris. Uncertain whether or not to read it now, I hold it loosely, weighing the pros and cons of opening it immediately. I hesitate, and then decide to wait until late afternoon—Jonas will be sketching then, and, as usual, I'll have tea out on the patio before dressing for the cocktail hour.

There is only one person, a young girl, swimming in the pool, lightly, playfully slapping the water. I glance at the plate of petit fours the waiter places on the table, but decide I will only drink tea, black, as I like it at this time of day. The white shorts and pale blue halter top I wear feel crisp and clean, constraining. Once the tray with teapot and cup is before me, I cross my legs and take a few sips. I rest the cup in the saucer and then intently open the letter; with a strange sense of excitement I peer down at Helen's fine, circular writing.

I read the first few paragraphs, studying each sentence. Then I stop and skim through the letter, intending to go back and read it more thoroughly a second time. Soon I have a sense of the gist of the letter; most importantly how much Helen has discerned about my relationship with the Sokolovs. Now, with care, I again read her words.

Tuscany
August 25

Dear Jenny,

I imagine you are surprised to hear from me—Helen, of all people, you think—or possibly not; maybe you have been expecting to receive news from Tuscany. Most who meet and share confidences while on holiday form a friendship during their short time together and agree to write once separated, but few do. We will be one of the exceptions, I trust. I often think of our parting ten days ago—you stood outside the hotel in the midday heat as Jonas helped Marc pack the car with our luggage. After you and I buckled Remy snugly into his car seat, you seemed faint from the strong sun but readily and graciously hugged me. I felt there was a sense of detachment in your warmth, or maybe "detachment" is the wrong word—perhaps "evasiveness" is better. Did you not want me to perceive something about you, or, maybe, in a subtle way, you did?

With the exception of a few cool evenings, the heat has been stifling since I have come to Roberto and Aunt Isa's Tuscan home, fertile ground for the imagination. I wonder if I should start at the beginning of my stay in Tuscany or work backward. I believe it is always best to write in an orderly way and then things will be more clear to you; knowing who I think you are, I believe you will prefer it this way.

We arrived at Roberto and Isa's home in Tuscany about six hours after we had said good-bye to you and Jonas. Remy slept most of the journey, and awoke with a start once Marc turned into the long driveway of their home. Cypress trees stood on either side of the path; riding over the dirt driveway, we could see in the distance a succession of green hills with spots of brown. The air was warm and soothing. Their stucco home is large with flower boxes in the front windows. I was surprised to see Aunt Isa sitting outside at a long table on the front side of the house. She wore a floppy white hat and an A-line white cotton dress. Just as we got out of the car my mother came to the front door. She ran down the steps to greet us, encircling the three of us in her arms, her glasses slipping to the end of her nose. Her movements are much quicker than Aunt Isa's, more svelte. Then after embracing us again, individually this time, and asking about our trip, she took Remy by the hand and led him up the front steps.

As I wiped my face with a handkerchief, Marc went over to speak with my aunt; she was reading a magazine. Looking up, she squinted and waved hello to him. When she saw me coming toward her she smiled curtly, but at the same time seemed pleased to see the two of us. She did not say much, responding nonchalantly to our small talk. I thought she might have been embarrassed by her behavior at the hotel. She told us she didn't expect Roberto to come for another three weeks and by then we would have left for our home in Paris. I responded that we had seen a good deal of Roberto at the hotel and I knew he was looking forward to coming to Tuscany once he had finished with his business meetings there. "Oh," she said, "Roberto, all business, all the time." Then in her hasty way, she instructed us to go inside, and said that Cira, my mother, would show us which rooms we would be staying in this time. As we began to turn away, she added that her son Caleb and Hans, his father, had driven to Florence and would not return until later in the evening. I felt less apprehensive after hearing her speak, and although she was not as welcoming as she was when we were children, she seemed more steady than she had at the hotel a few weeks before. I was relieved, hoping the visit would be more pleasant than expected.

Over dinner Aunt Isa was more talkative, and my mother was quiet; she had prepared dinner and had spent much time engaging Remy with food and a game of hide-and-seek while Marc and I had slipped off for a nap after our drive from the Riviera.

That evening Aunt Isa was fussy about what she ate and drank, and I don't know if now she was adhering to her doctor's orders. For I not only did not know what ails her, I did not know what she needs to do to protect her health. But she appeared more even-tempered than she had on the Riviera, where she had been tense and had been drinking too much, acting out in ways that had been extreme, even for her.

As we enjoyed dessert, mille-feuille, *my mother's specialty, Aunt Isa spoke of those years when my sisters and I were young and would come to visit America, how we had been awed by New York and the tall buildings. She said it had struck her as curious each time we had come, as she had thought Paris to be quite sophisticated; we'd acted like girls who never before had been within miles of a city. It was then*

I noticed she was not wearing her wedding ring; I supposed it was because Caleb would soon return. He does not like ostentatious jewelry, and since her marriage to Roberto, Aunt Isa tries to appease Caleb.

Caleb has a closer relationship with his father than he does with his mother; Uncle Hans and he are more compatible—it is not surprising that Caleb has chosen the same profession as his father. I understand that Caleb, despite his awareness of Aunt Isa's flaws, her unpredictable personality, which became more and more evident the older he grew, feels a deep warmth toward his mother at certain times and on other occasions appears annoyed with her. As an adult he will be happy to see her when they have been apart for a while, and then after too many days together he will appear resolute in leaving her until the next visit. He has not acknowledged this to me but I have closely observed Caleb—as I am the older cousin I have felt protective of him and because of this I think I know him quite well. I am confident Caleb would wholeheartedly agree with what I am relaying to you, Jenny.

Although Aunt Isa was talkative during the meal, the rest of us were more subdued than usual. Remy sat next to my mother and she helped him eat and spoke to him gently, asking him questions about our vacation on the Riviera. My sisters and their husbands and daughters had not yet arrived, and were expected to come early the next morning. Even though Marc and I had taken a nap, we were still weary from the drive. It was pleasant to see Aunt Isa in good spirits, telling story after story of the people who lived in this small Tuscan village and how American she felt in their company. Wasn't it ironic, she said, that she had been born in Trieste?

"America is compelling," she added, "the culture is transformative." But I think Aunt Isa must have always been comfortable in the United States, for she had seemed very American to me—no different in this way from her first husband and son. But now she was married to Roberto, I thought, who, like herself, had been born in Trieste.

Even at a young age I had wondered how stable Aunt Isa was. I had never liked being alone with her, as she could say something unexpected and jarring. Or she'd be suddenly alarmed about an occurrence that even as a child I understood was innocuous, but then at the next moment she'd be calm and practical and continue on with her plans for the day. She was different from most other adults I knew, and sometimes I would look over at Caleb and wonder what it was like for him. Yet he seemed indifferent, apparently accustomed to her behavior, and when I was young I accepted his response. But eventually, I realized how difficult it must be for him.

Out of the blue, Aunt Isa sighed, her expression more melancholic. She put down her fork and said emphatically, "Roberto is angry with me; he said I was too boisterous the last night I was at the hotel, but I don't think so. Perhaps I had too much wine, though I never did become intoxicated, just ebullient, I guess you could say."

My mother turned to her and said, "You become much too excited, Isa, over meaningless things. Situations and people in general are not always how you imagine them to be. It is as if you are looking at life through a mirror that causes a person to appear misshapen. Hans was a wonderful man but you envisioned him differently; in your head you invented images of him that were not true. He is a much better person than you believe him to be—or maybe you wanted him to become a negative force in your life because you needed to divorce him so you could marry Roberto."

I have heard my mother express such thoughts before, especially during dinners with only my aunt and herself and Marc and me. She does not speak to Aunt Isa in this way when my father or sisters and their husbands are present. When Aunt Isa is in Paris or when we visit her, my sisters never pay as much attention to her as Marc and I do. For some reason we are more drawn to her than are other family members. Roberto, I gather, detests Aunt Isa's unpleasant moods, but when she is bright and spirited, he relishes her.

Over coffee, we were mostly silent, weary from a long day, but soon heard the shutting of car doors, then steps in the foyer, and shortly Caleb and Uncle Hans came into the dining room.

I had not seen Caleb in two years, and now that he would be thirty in a few months, he appeared more like Hans than before. His expression was more serious than I remembered and he was thinner, his face more narrow and defined; he had grown a faint mustache. I was curious to know what his life had been like these past few years.

Uncle Hans appeared the same as always; he never seems to change very much. Aunt Isa waved to him briefly, as if shooing him away. Although she had invited Uncle Hans to her and Roberto's home in Tuscany, she did so to ensure that Caleb would visit.

My mother offered to serve them dinner. They were appreciative, as they had come upon traffic driving back from Florence, where they had met a former colleague of Uncle Hans's, and then had spent some time at the Uffizi Gallery. Florence suits them; according to Caleb, it is where in Europe they are most at ease, especially since Uncle Hans and Aunt Isa's divorce.

Over the osso buco *that my mother had adroitly placed before them, they spoke about a painting at the gallery, attributed to Francesco Furini,* Portrait of a Young Girl, *saying that although it was dated 1650, her expression is surprisingly modern. Aunt Isa looked at them quizzically, as if she could not understand their interest in the work—or was it that she found their description of the painting too frank and uninspired?*

It was close to midnight when we got up from the table. As we were leaving the room, Aunt Isa approached Caleb and put her arms around him. From the hallway I heard her ask if he would stay with her for a while so that they could catch up. Her tone was more subdued than usual but she sounded motherly and sincere. I looked back and saw him smile uncertainly. I could see his fondness for her and at the same time there was a subtle wariness in his look. But I saw and heard no more; soon we had reached the top of the stairway. Marc was carrying Remy, who was sleeping, in his arms, and I went ahead to open the door of our bedroom.

The next day I came upon Uncle Hans in the study. He would be staying until Monday, and Caleb would be leaving two days later, on Wednesday. It was early afternoon, a Saturday, and my sisters and their husbands and daughters had arrived that morning. I had just come inside; reverberating through my mind and body were the sounds of the girls splashing water in the pool and their screams of joy. Remy had been sitting on Marc's lap, gleefully watching his older cousins frolicking. When I walked into the study, Uncle Hans was lounging on the sofa. He immediately stood and greeted me. He appeared distracted and I believed he was lost in thought about something that was disturbing him. I know how dedicated he is to his work and guessed he was concerned about patients of his. He asked how I was, and together we tried to determine when it was we had last met. I addressed him as Uncle Hans as I always had—for was he not the father of my dear cousin Caleb? We concluded we had last seen each other in Paris two years before. He and Caleb had been attending a conference and I had invited them to dinner at our apartment. Remy had not yet begun to walk. We sat across from each other; the curtains were open and light flooded the room. In the distance I could see a small group of people walking toward the grassy hills.

Uncle Hans mentioned he had been to Roberto's hotel on the Riviera. "I heard you and Marc were there at the time. My stay was brief—one night. I was meeting friends in Genoa the next day. I did not have a chance to contact you, but knew I would see you in Tuscany. I heard a couple nearly drowned the night before."

As he spoke, it struck me that his purpose in going there might have been to see Mara. I have always found Uncle Hans to be a person who keeps his feelings at a distance. I don't think he would have wanted to be questioned about her. Instead I spoke of Aunt Isa, telling him she appeared more stable in Tuscany, and explained her behavior at the hotel, how she had erupted at dinner. And then I told him about you, Jenny. What might have contributed to Aunt Isa's behavior that night—according to what she had told Roberto—was that at the next table she recognized a woman her husband refers to as Jenny Stram, her maiden name, Smila.

Uncle Hans smiled and said, "The name Smila is familiar." Then he crossed his legs, leaned his head back as if searching his memory. After a few moments, he said, "I know of her through her mother, who once was a patient of mine. I probably should not reveal this, but it has been so many years. She would come with her mother to New York to see me—they lived in Connecticut, Hartford, I recall, but when they moved away I lost touch with them. The young daughter would stay in the waiting room while her mother would come in to see me. I don't believe she would recognize me—a nurse would accompany her mother into my office. Her mother would tell me that her young daughter was in the waiting room. I remember more clearly now. Often we would talk about Caleb and her daughter once we realized they were the same age. From my office window I would see them climbing up the front steps of the brownstone. Her mother was born in Trieste like your mother and aunt, and that is why I remember her—because of that coincidence. And even before she was my patient, Isa and I may have gone to a party at their apartment in Hartford, a party mostly for immigrants from Trieste, but that was too long ago to remember for certain; it is very vague and it may be that Isa only talked of herself going. And now that you say she is staying at the hotel, I may have seen her on the Riviera. I knew I had seen her before; she has the same face as she did as a twelve- or thirteen-year-old girl. Even though she was quite young, there was something old about her. And the same expression—it is haunting. It is coming back to me now. Maybe it is why Isa, who tends to respond emotionally rather than thinking first, reacted to seeing her in that way. I think Isa tried to befriend her once and I had advised her against doing so because of my past professional contact with her mother, but I did so more because I was concerned that Isa would not be a good influence on her. But I probably did not need to say anything to Isa; you know she is not the most consistent of friends and she was much older than her. And so I may have seen her again in New York when she was in her early twenties."

At that moment Remy ran into the room, soaking wet from having been in the pool, and jumped onto my lap, clutching at me in a wet hug.

Uncle Hans left a few days later, and I did not have another chance to speak with him alone. Coming upon him following our talk, he would seem preoccupied and distant as if we had not had conversed that day, but whenever he caught my eye he would smile thoughtfully. His time in Tuscany was spent mostly with Caleb; they would swim in the evening and speak alone together in the study after dinner. Uncle Hans left Tuscany on Monday, midday. Caleb drove him to the airport.

I did not have a chance to talk alone with Caleb until the night before he left. During most of his stay he had enjoyed playing with my sisters' daughters and with Remy. I had not seen that side of Caleb before and wondered if he were considering having children of his own. He seemed more delighted by his second cousins than he had in the past. They all called him Uncle Caleb.

The windows remained open and throughout the house there was a sense of early autumn. Remy had fallen asleep over dessert. Marc held him in his arms for most of the dinner, and after we finished our meal, he carried him upstairs to our room. When Marc did not reappear, I assumed he had fallen asleep alongside our son.

After dinner I went in to the study to look for a book to read. Although the others were tired from the change in the weather, I was restless and needed to occupy my mind. As I was looking through the shelves, I heard footsteps. Turning, I saw that Caleb had come into the room, a glass of wine in his hand. He offered to get me one as well. And soon we were sitting across from each other, lounging in big stuffy chairs, my legs tucked beneath me. We had always enjoyed talking with each other, and it was easy to take up where we had left off two years before. I told him I had noticed his sudden interest in the children and hadn't seen that side of him before. "Is there something more to it?" I asked.

He shrugged. "I am not involved with anyone now, Helen, if that is what you are asking," he said, smiling.

"You will be thirty in October; that is how old I was when Marc and I married. Maybe there is someone you are interested in but you do not realize it yet," I said, teasing him.

What I gathered from Caleb was that he had been overworking lately, and seeing the children and enjoying time with them had been his way of unwinding, diverting himself from the burdens of his career. Both he and Uncle Hans only treat trauma cases; that has always been Uncle Hans's specialty. I can only imagine how exhausting it must be. They are both in practice together now. I asked him about his father, if he thought he would remarry at some point. Caleb then told me that Uncle Hans had stopped by to visit Mara when he was on the Riviera, and although they were happy to see each other, his father had said that there was a distance between them. Caleb closed his eyes and told me this was because they blamed each other for the failure of their respective marriages.

"Yes, Caleb," I said, "people like to blame themselves; ironically it makes them feel less guilty. I met a woman on the beach at the hotel, her name is Jenny, and I thought she blamed herself for her first husband's death—he died tragically, in a yachting accident—his name was Eric Stram. He was from Trieste; he had worked for Roberto—that was how she had known about the hotel."

Caleb's gaze met mine, and there was silence. I was surprised and uncomfortable. After a while, he simply said, "There was a time when I knew her well." At that moment the tension between us lessened some.

"She is married to an artist now, a talented one, I think, who is also kind and surprisingly brave," I answered, and Caleb seemed pleased, but then we discussed other things.

I am not certain what your relationship was with my cousin, or the year or years you were in contact with each other; you now have both moved on—haven't you?

Your friend,
Helen

Eleven

The Response

I do not reflect much on Helen's letter, realizing I need to respond while still in the surroundings in which she and I met and exchanged confidences. For once we each return to our respective homes, our day-to-day lives will resume, and the mystique of our vacation on the Riviera will fade away.

Early the next morning, while sipping coffee at the patio café, I watch Jonas swimming in the pool close by. The water is an aqua color; his strokes are even and strong, the movement of his head, left, right, left, right. Then I look out a short distance at the Mediterranean, the glinting sunlight crossing its breadth. I pick up my pen and close my eyes; I need to write the truth. What I glean most from Helen's words is not that I did not reveal to her the depth of my relationship with her cousin Caleb, but that I neglected to mention I had known of him. My intention was not to be deceptive, just protective of Caleb's privacy and mine. But after reading her letter, I realize I was mistaken; I should have told her. Secondly I was disoriented by the news that for a time, while we lived in Hartford, Hans Sokolov had been my mother's physician. Eighteen hours later, I am still puzzled by this information. My instinct is the friendship Helen and I have begun to develop will not survive.

Jonas is the only one in the pool. As I begin to write, I hear the sound of his arms slapping water.

The Riviera
August 28

Dear Helen,

I realize you must be home in Paris by now—perhaps you have just returned and are still under the warm spell of your summer trip.

I was not surprised to receive your letter, but disturbed by its contents. You are very perceptive, Helen—I understood this about you when we first spoke on the beach, and I noticed you were reading Céline's Journey to the End of the Night, *a novel, I believe, that is enjoyed by those who tend to be contemplative, questioning, and responsive to life.*

And as I attempt to imagine the light in which you may view what I say, I weigh in my mind what to reveal about my relationship with your cousin Caleb. I realize what is most important is that you continue to think well of him. What I write will be with that purpose in mind. It is not helpful, I think, for you to have too many unanswered questions about your cousin, questions that may arouse doubts that affect your genuine appreciation of him. And although you see each other every so often, maybe once every two years, it is enough, it sounds, to maintain a close relationship.

I met Caleb seven years ago; it was a transitional time for each of us, or at least for me—I will not speak for him. That summer I became enthralled with the Sokolov family. The months of July and August were extremely hot and I was feeling listless and uncertain about my life, the choices I had made. My husband Eric was away for many of those weeks.

I met your aunt Isa first. It was during a heavy downpour; we stood beneath the awning of a clothing store on Madison Avenue, waiting for the rain to subside. After a while, to help pass the time, we began to converse. When she discovered I was thinking of a career in journalism, she offered to introduce me to an acquaintance of hers, who was a professor in the field. I was surprised by her openness and desire to assist, and since I was lonely in New York and unhappy in my marriage, I was hopeful and pleased by the idea of seeing her again to discuss this possibility. However, my next meeting with your aunt, two days later, a Saturday morning, turned out to be an abrupt and disorienting encounter. Her personality was very different when we first met. Her husband Hans soon joined us and he was indifferent to me as well. I had no idea he had been my mother's doctor. I remember when I was young and we were living in Hartford, I would often take the train with my mother to New York and accompany her to medical appointments. But I do not remember Hans. My mother has always been inclined to visit doctors, specialists, even for minor health issues. However, it is true that seven years ago I was drawn to Hans. Hans was the Sokolov I found most compelling. Maybe it was because unknowingly I had seen him at one point when I was young, and memories I was unaware of had been in some way reawakened, evoking a sense of familiarity. I found there was something both warm and mysterious about Hans and Caleb—their relationship, I mean.

You write that Hans's specialty has always been trauma, but I know of no personal trauma my mother might have experienced, nor am I aware of any apparent neurological deficit she might have had. I was young at the time and not very observant of either of my parents. I tended to focus primarily on my future, what would happen once we left Hartford; my parents would often speak of moving away. This was what was foremost in my mind; I was both excited and apprehensive about leaving Hartford, the only place I had known.

My mother is and always has been a complicated person. My father has been called heroic. As I mentioned to you on the beach he was an anti-fascist; he had taken part in dangerous activities—in opposition to Mussolini—in Trieste, which I had not been aware of until Eric informed me. I married Eric because his family had protected my parents during the war. My mother has never been straightforward about any matter, and once I was mature enough to understand her behavior, I attributed it to her experience during the war. I can only imagine how difficult the time must have been for those living in Europe. I do not know if your mother has spoken of those years.

I did not see my parents during the months I knew Caleb—they had spent a good deal of time in Trieste that summer and remained there through the fall. Although Eric had encouraged me to go with them, I had decided against doing so; I had not wanted them to know our marriage was an unsuccessful one. Naturally they would have realized this if I had visited Trieste with them and had not planned to see my husband later while he at the time was in Italy on business. For Eric had led me to believe he did not want to meet in Europe that summer, that he intended to keep his distance.

Caleb had completed his medical school coursework the previous spring. Hans was attempting to set him up in an exchange program in Amsterdam. I do not believe Hans was aware of my relationship with Caleb. It might have been a difficult time for him as well—for I gathered that Isa had begun to spend much time away from Hans and Caleb. It was a time of uneasiness for all, and as I said, the heat was relentless, seemingly inescapable, our limitations both practical and psychological preventing us from exiting the city.

When Caleb and I first spoke, he did not realize I was married, and by the time I told him it was too late; we had become close very soon after meeting. Before he left for Europe, he told me I needed to make a decision about my marriage. I would have preferred to have continued on in secret, but Caleb did not agree. While he was in Amsterdam he wrote and asked several times if I had made a decision. As I repeatedly avoided his question, he eventually stopped contacting me. And so your cousin Caleb remained honest and ethical; he always wanted to do what was right and fair and I wish him only the best, as I had put him in an untenable position from the start. But you must understand I did not do so in a calculated way or willingly. I simply could not leave Eric; I felt bound to him and it was an awful feeling. It was as if I were in a jail of sorts, a self-imposed one—for I could have walked away; no one would have stopped me. Maybe it was related to Eric's nightmares; he had horrible dreams because of the war and I felt responsible for him in that way. He had been harmed because of what he had witnessed, I believed. As Roberto asked, "Why did little Eric not speak?" After some thought, I now wonder if Roberto may know the answer.

Eric never spoke of his experiences as a child during the war, and whenever I questioned him about those years, he would not answer; he'd become angry—not openly, but I could feel hostility brewing within him. I was never frightened of Eric but I was frightened for him, what he might do that would cause him to become more flawed, more withdrawn. For I had gathered that we would eventually part—we had not been intimate in over a year—things could not go on as they were.

When I miscarried, it was, of course, Caleb's baby. Eric did not ask questions, pretending it was his when both of us knew it was impossible. I do not think it disturbed him that I had been involved with someone else—I think he was that confused. How was it possible for me to leave someone who was lost? I was waiting until he found himself in some way—then I would be able to go on with my life, then I could leave. But I was compelled; I could not separate from Eric until this began to happen. At the time I could not explain this to Caleb, as I had not fully realized it myself.

You must be convinced I treated your cousin terribly, but I did not purposely do so. Caleb was searching for some sort of comfort that summer. He was disillusioned with his mother—he eventually told me he was vaguely aware she was having an affair with someone on the Riviera—and he was angry with his father for his lack of assertiveness, allowing Isa to leave the both of them for long periods of time. And Caleb was looking, I believe, for a distraction, a way to soothe himself, and I was there and I was good to him—that was, until he left for Amsterdam.

I believe Caleb was right to end our relationship, and I made the correct decision to stay with my husband. My regret is that I was not able to help Eric.

I never told Caleb about the miscarriage. Would he have wanted to know? I find it painful that you speak of his playing with the children. If my pregnancy had continued, would not our child have been six years old now? Close to the age of one of your sisters' daughters? But the pregnancy ceased and Eric died three years later. And so in essence nothing of significance had been gained.

Although I knew Jonas was in New York at the time, and had seen him occasionally at the gallery where he worked, he was simply a friend. Before I met Caleb I had hoped to have a relationship with Jonas; he wasn't interested because I was married. I did not see him with any regularity until after

Eric's passing. He had come to me to extend his sympathy. And eventually and slowly we became involved. He encouraged me not to feel guilty about Eric's death and coaxed me out of my mourning. Of the two of us, I was the one who was looking for a romantic relationship. Jonas was hesitant because he was only beginning to feel confident as an artist and wasn't certain how successful he would be financially. He also was unsure about becoming involved in a committed relationship; his father had died before he was born, and Cora, his mother, had kept him from knowing her lover—and for those reasons he believed marriage was beyond him; he had not witnessed a mature relationship.

I did not tell Jonas about Caleb. I do not think he would have wanted to know. Though I believe he would have been understanding and would be today if I told him about my involvement with your cousin. Jonas was always aware that Eric and I were not compatible; as a friend and neighbor he accepted my decision to marry Eric and never caused me to question it. I trusted Jonas because I had known him longer than the other men I was acquainted with; he had never been dishonest with me, nor had he ever attempted to intrude in my life.

It has taken me this long to realize that Eric would never have been happy—it had to do with his temperament, I think. But I am not certain, I do not know what he experienced during the war. As his wife all I was aware of was how he would cry out from his nightmares. I would awaken and try to soothe him. Only when he was half-conscious would he let me do so.

If I had not been so young when we met and married, I would have asked him directly about his dreams and maybe he would have been more forthcoming about his past. Perhaps he would have revealed what he had experienced and I could have helped him resolve it in some way. I simply do not know and will never know—it is something I will live with always, but as the years pass, the burden is lighter; time allows you to see that one person cannot solve all problems or be everything to any one, even one's spouse. We all have a responsibility to improve our lives. It is up to the individual, I think. Yet I understand I will always believe that to a certain extent I contributed to Eric's sadness. Living with an unhappy person causes you to become melancholic and then you act in ways you would not have before you met him.

I have enjoyed speaking to Mara the few times I have gone to her shop. She has given me a perspective on my own life, one that was needed, and to a degree, she has helped me sort things out.

As I told you on the beach, Jonas and I came to Roberto's hotel because of the postcard I discovered this past June, one that Eric had sent me before we became involved. There was nothing of significance in his words, but the picture on the front of the card was of the hotel. In coming to the Riviera I was hoping to find some justification in my marriage to Eric—it has been my way of mourning him—but this visit has only unearthed more questions than answers. I brought the postcard with me, but I have misplaced it, which is probably for the best.

I hope my letter has eased your doubts.

Your loyal friend,
Jenny

Twelve

The Dream

On the thirtieth of August, Jonas and I motor toward the Nice airport; the drive is easy, the car windows fully open, the morning breeze soft, caressing. I look back and take a last glimpse; once we turn the next corner the hotel will no longer be in sight. What comes to mind as it has many times over this month is how the exterior of the building, utilitarian in concept and odd in structure, is markedly inconsequential in contrast to the exquisite foliage and the all-encompassing vista of the glistening Mediterranean.

We will take a quick flight to Paris and from there we'll board a plane to New York. It is early and there are only a few other cars on the road. Off to the right we pass a series of stone walls and an abundance of magenta-colored bougainvillea.

As we near the airport, I am stricken with a sense of loss. Many questions linger; I understand that I may never fully comprehend the memory that has become part of me, haunting me; it may never cease doing so.

I did not say good-bye to Mara and have not seen her since the day Hans walked into her café. I had slipped away before she realized I'd left. I strain to keep in memory that image of her—the moment her eyes fastened on Hans, her lips parted, the contours of her face, accentuated, hardened, reflecting her passion for him, her eyes expressing her fear of it.

Six hours have passed since we left the hotel. At the Paris airport now, about to board the plane to New York, we wait in line, our shoulders touching. Jonas takes my arm and I turn to him, his eyes are set; he asks if I am happy about having come to the Riviera. There is a yearning tone in his voice, which confuses me. I nod. And then to deflect his serious mood, I tease him, tell him I am surprised he has not shown me his sketches. Grinning briefly, he shrugs. As we file onto the plane, I sense his unease.

An hour into the flight we drink wine, a red musky liquid, lingering in the throat. When I ask Jonas to describe his drawings, he speaks evasively, vaguely referring to the Mediterranean, the foliage. He does not say which ones, if any, will become paintings, which works he will discard, or just keep as sketches. In his shirt pocket there is a small box filled with sticks of pastels. When I ask about them, he says he purchased the pastels because they remind him of the colors of the Riviera.

Feeling loosened from the wine, in exaggerated detail I begin to describe the memory that has been haunting me. Fervently, I say it has become a part of me; it burdens me, prevents me from being completely free.

He takes my hand but does not speak of my memory; instead, he responds, "Jenny, I encouraged you not to mourn for Eric, I hoped to distance you from that feeling—you were too young to be sad."

As he speaks, I watch him closely. Although there may be truth in what he is saying, I do not reflect on his words, more on his demeanor. How he raises his brows when he speaks, the turn of his head, revealing the sharp angle of his face, his high forehead, his hand clutching mine, long fingers, wiry, active hands, not passive, but he is mostly calm and assured, how he rests his shoulders against the chair, how he spaces his words.

Then he turns away as if to gather his thoughts. When he again faces me, he says, "This memory you have been speaking of—is it real? Or is it a conflation of bits and pieces of occurrences in your life from many years ago and perhaps even from the recent past? Maybe they have all fused in your mind to create this memory. Maybe it did not happen in the way you recall; perhaps it is a dream, a recurring one you had when you were a child—or, could it have to do with . . ." He pauses and then says, "Eric."

I look directly at him and say honestly, "But Jonas, I never think of Eric, unless I am forced to."

His voice is caressing, yet I hear a touch of irritation in it. I know he does not want to sound mean or hurtful, "Who forces you, Jenny?"

"I force myself, Jonas, whenever I am reminded of him, who else would?"

"Roberto?" he asks.

"Roberto doesn't faze me. I do not believe him, his words. I think he invents what he says; he is unreliable."

"Roberto is complex," Jonas answers.

Then he smiles as he does whenever he intends to change the subject. He tells me about one of the waiters at the hotel, how he had asked him if he'd like to buy a watch. Understanding it was a joke, he went along with him—I do not need a watch, Jonas told him. But you will when you are home, the waiter said, and pointed to me as I approached the table. You will need to watch her when you go back to America. I laugh. We laugh together at the silly joke. Soon, drowsy from the wine and the hum of the engines, I turn away, and before I fall asleep, I look over at Jonas and my gaze catches the box of pastels in his shirt pocket. Reflexively, I lower the flap of material to cover them, my fingers graze the powdery sticks; my eyelids heavy, lowering against my will.

The box of pastels is larger now, the size of a window. You reach over to touch it as if it were a pane, but the sticks begin to melt from the strong sunlight. The colors pour out, staining the glass. A hand presses your shoulder, but when you turn round no one is there. You become fearful. In the distance you see Hans coming toward you. You are on the street now. He stays at a distance, does not look at you. As he approaches, you realize it is not Hans but Caleb, and suddenly he seems more at a distance, and disappears. Did he go inside a house? There are many homes—you do not know which one it is; you feel discouraged. Tears flow down your face. As you begin to walk home, you bump into Helen—or is it Mara? They appear similar in every way, even age, though you know Mara is more than twenty years older. Your dispiritedness turns to frustration. You look upward and see the window that was Jonas's box of pastels; the pane is now red. Someone is opening it—Eric sticks out his head and nods at you; he does not wave but nods. You stand on your toes and wave, but looking up, you see he is no longer there. Instead it is Roberto, staring out with his hawklike gaze, and behind him is Mara—or is it Isa? Now you find yourself in New York—your apartment, but no, it is another apartment, the one in Hartford maybe, and you are alone, no one else is here. You hear your mother crying out for you. It is very cold, no more sun. You are shivering and alone in the apartment; there is no heat. There is no furniture other than one chair against the wall. You go and sit on it, crossing your arms, rubbing them with your hands to keep yourself warm. Eric walks by in a rush, does not see you. You cry out, tell him you are cold. He is gone. Hans and Caleb walk in attached at the shoulder; they are naked and their expressions are in opposition, as if one is wearing a mask of tragedy and the other of comedy, but you cannot determine who is wearing which one. Jonas comes in; he stands in front of a gate. You are outdoors now; it is warm but you are still in the chair. He opens the gate and swiftly approaches Hans and Caleb; placing one hand on each of their shoulders, he attempts to pull them apart. You watch without feeling. You know Jonas but not as much as you will know him. Soon he disappears and so do Hans and Caleb.

Inside the room again, you are more cold than you were. You shiver; still sitting in the chair, you realize you are glued to it. But looking out the window across the room you see it is warm and sunny. Your parents come to the window and wave from outside, your mother blowing kisses in that stolid way of hers, your father subtly smiling. He is pleased with your mother, with you, with himself, but it is not obvious; people do not realize, do not know him. He is more confident than he seems. But suddenly it becomes dark as if night has come. You no longer see your parents. You do not know if they are still outside the window or if they have left. But soon you realize you are alone, as if you have been alone the entire time; you feel separate from those you have seen—they have not made an impression on you.

Slowly coming into consciousness, you are unable to raise your eyelids; they are glued to your sockets as you are to the chair. For you are still half in your dream, one you cannot leave. Caleb returns, but not Hans. He is not alone; he is holding something in his arms, a baby with blond hair. Abruptly Caleb and the infant vanish. Not able to move from the chair, still stuck to it, you look down; at your feet is a pool of blood.

My lashes wet, I open my eyes and hear the uneven sound of Jonas's voice as if he's been roused from his sleep, telling me we have almost arrived; over the intercom I hear a voice telling us to straighten our seats. As I press the button to do so, I look down and smile, but then I am uneasy—for what I thought I lost has been found; on my lap is the postcard from Eric.

Thirteen

The Return

The day after our return, the last of August, the heat is dry and piercing, no hint of a breeze. In the grassy area behind the apartment building, Jonas and I rest beneath the shade of the willow tree. His head presses against the trunk; I lie across his lap, my back against his shifting knees. Surrounding us are clusters of daisies, limp and spaced apart, nearly hidden by the overgrown grass. Weary from traveling, we are mostly silent.

A streak of light passing through an opening in the fine branches is blinding. I shield my eyes with one hand and slightly lift my head; Jonas comes close, anticipating my words. A ray crosses the side of his face, revealing a glint of green in his dark-eyed gaze, a suggestion of mild sarcasm at the corner of his mouth, a purposefulness in the line of his jaw.

"Jenny?" he asks promptly, willing me to speak.

I lie back again, my head touching the dry grass, my heart beats rapidly. Flushed from the warmth of the sun, I eye the drifting, wispy clouds, and then raise my head, bringing my face near his. "You want to know about the postcard," I say, peering into his eyes.

Blinking, his lashes long and sparse, his words measured, "How long have you had it?"

"Only a few months." I sit up, now facing him, empowered by my need to reveal. "I found it in my parents' home, in my bedroom, in a book, one that I read a few times the summer I met you, months before I became involved with Eric. I had used the postcard as a bookmark, I suppose. When I discovered it in June, I had not remembered receiving it—it drew a blank in my memory. And I thought the hotel might be interesting to go to. I was not aware that once on the Riviera, figures would emerge from the past."

"You really did not know Roberto's second wife," Jonas says, his voice edgy, "and his ex-wife is from Eric's past, not yours. You had heard of Roberto but did not know him, did not even remember his name."

I shrug and say, "There is more, Jonas."

He lowers his head, does not raise it; I speak candidly about Isa and Hans and Caleb and Helen—I add that I had not met Helen until this summer; I had not known that Caleb had a cousin who lived in Paris. For he had only vaguely mentioned cousins in Europe—not naming a particular country—and said he would stop by and visit with them once he finished with the exchange program in Amsterdam.

Jonas's head remains lowered, I cannot read his expression, do not know how he is interpreting or comprehending what I am telling him. He's wearing khaki shorts, his legs slightly open, his knees up, his palms on the grass. An ant circling his shin is nearly camouflaged by the hair on his legs. I cannot intuit what he is thinking, feeling—he doesn't want me to—I continue on as it is what he desires; he needs to hear, to know.

When I speak of Caleb, I wonder if Jonas is uncertain—will I be loyal to him as I was not to Eric? This is important to him—Jonas lives by a strict ethical code. My guess is he will surmise that if I believed I was unhappy in my marriage I should have left, perhaps even married Caleb, been honest about it with Eric, with myself—but these are only guesses. I continue, sometimes hesitantly, sometimes warmly, sometimes uncertainly, but invariably honestly.

The more I explain, the stronger I feel, the more compassion I have for Jonas, and at the same time, the more angry I am with him for not having realized what may have occurred during my marriage to Eric.

When I finish, there is silence, not an empty silence, but one filled with apprehension, frustration, anger, and passion—each of us inwardly experiencing these emotions, maybe not in the same order, but with the same intensity. Yet there is an ironic side to Jonas, which he may very well express momentarily. But I am older now, accepting of his flaws, my own, and those of others, comprehending that I come face to face with one or more of them every time I converse with a person or eye myself in the mirror.

Jonas speaks first. He does not raise his head and I am reminded of when I first met him that summer, my eighteenth, the August I received Eric's postcard, that when I approached Jonas, his head had remained lowered, and that he had not raised it until after he had introduced himself. Then when he lifted his gaze, I had been struck by the complexity in his penetrating dark eyes and, as young and inexperienced as I was, I understood he possessed a perspective and knowledge of the world that was quite foreign to me, one that I might never desire to comprehend. At that moment, I was endeared to him. Though I had realized all this about him on that day, I never could have foreseen our evolution as friends, lovers, and eventually a married couple.

"Jenny," he now says, and in his tone I hear concern, hurt, and longing, but not distrust or irony, the way he may sound at his darkest moments. "You did not need to say everything; it wasn't necessary." But when our gazes meet, I see he is uncomfortable about what I have revealed to him, uncertain whether or not it will bother him in the long term. Yet I believe he is relieved I have been this forthcoming. Maybe he knows he can trust me now. Though I am not looking for his trust or acceptance.

Because of our jet lag, we go to bed early. In the middle of the night Jonas calls out in his sleep. I sit up and lean close to him, hoping to hear what he is saying—it is a muddle of words: Eric, Cora, Caleb—as if he's speaking of one person.

I lie down again and try to sleep. I glance at the clock. It is 2 a.m., a new day, a new month, September, realizing summer is slipping away; with a slight feeling of melancholy, I already miss the intensity of August. Different thoughts wander through my mind, fleeting images—Mara, sitting in her shop, an unlit cigarette dangling between two fingers, her expression enigmatic, or Helen, her head lowered, fingering the edges of her floppy hat. I envision Hans, his expression a blend of wistfulness and dispassion as he came into Mara's shop, as well as Roberto lifting his chin and asking, "Why did young Eric not speak?" his hawklike eyes evading my gaze. But I am not thinking of the memory that dominated most of the summer, that passionately clung to me, haunting me—the man in the charcoal-colored pants swiftly passing me, a woman sitting in a chair with a red stain on her lap. For it strikes me now that it has lost its significance; it is not important anymore. I do not know if it was real or imagined or pieces of my past life from different experiences, out of sequence, folded into one memory. All I know is it no longer resonates within me; it is no longer there as a warning, or a burden I carry. There is no depth or mystery to the image I have broken apart and played over and over in my mind.

Fourteen

The Sketches

Ten years have passed since the August we spent at Roberto's hotel. Although Jonas and I have not returned, we have visited other places on the Riviera, pointedly avoiding the French-Italian border area and any city or town in close proximity to Mr. Carini's establishment.

I have not heard from or seen Roberto or Mara, or Helen and Marc; neither have I come across Hans or Caleb in New York, which is not surprising given the size and sprawling nature of the city, and how many of its inhabitants yearn for anonymity. Yet every year since that summer of ten years ago, some time in the heat of August, I have recalled our visit to the hotel. In certain years I have done so thoughtfully and on others, when I've been preoccupied with work or busy with practical matters, I have only fleetingly remembered the people I met and who in one way or another afforded me insight into my first husband, and also, though less significantly, the Sokolov family. In those years when my focus was contemplative, I arrived at different conclusions, each with the same intensity. The summers that my interest was superficial, my analysis was swift, equal to the short amount of time I spent thinking of them. The mystery or confusion of that August, I decided, had to do with the fact that I was not aware that Hans Sokolov had been my mother's doctor and that she had gone to him for behavioral neurological therapy—for that is what I have surmised. Given that her husband, my father, had worked in opposition to the government during the 1940s, the stress of it may have caused an assault on her nervous system, and naturally Eric, a child at the time, must have been scarred by events surrounding the war. In terms of Roberto, I concluded he was simply an aging man attempting to arrange the past in his mind, more for practical, cognitive reasons than with any depth.

On those August days when I thought more deeply about the summer of 1984, I'd replay in my mind the details that have stayed with me—my conversation with Helen on the beach, the novel she was reading, how tightly she gripped it, her mouth tense and awed, the magenta-colored bougainvillea surrounding the front of the hotel, Roberto standing next to the pool in the early morning hours, his fixed expression. What had he been contemplating? What had he experienced? How much did he know about my parents, how much did he know of Eric? As the years have passed, more and more I have believed he understood very well why little Eric did not speak, and that asking the question had been his way of gauging my knowledge.

After we returned to New York, our life together took its natural course. Jonas submerged himself in his work, and gradually his paintings garnered recognition from his colleagues. Once critics became interested in his work, art dealers did so as well. It was a slow process, but then suddenly, about three years ago, his name became recognized in that world.

The spring following that summer on the Riviera, I completed my master's degree in journalism—seven and a half years after I'd first contemplated doing so. After two years of freelance journalism, I found a job with a magazine that suited me.

The name of the magazine is *Life and Times*; it presents a cultural and psychological look at the world we live in today. It has a small but consistent following and

I am not paid very much for the articles I write, but I am content with my work. I meet interesting people and have enjoyed interviewing each one of them, discovering their purpose in life, why they have chosen to do what they do. I have traveled to different parts of the country as well as to various nations.

Jonas and I have often been apart; I need to be away a good amount of time—occasionally he'll accompany me, especially if there is a particular landscape or site he wants to see or if it is a place he has never been. One time he came with me because there was an art exhibit he wanted to view in London, where I would be interviewing an antique dealer—it was about seven years ago, the first year I began writing for the magazine. The dealer had red hair cut short and styled—Jonas and I saw her through the front window before walking into her store, we looked at each other, silently wondering if she was the woman on the beach Jonas had attempted to save from drowning. She appeared eerily like her. And during the interview, whenever I questioned her about her work or one of her items, the way she raised her eyebrows with surprise yet absence was hauntingly familiar. Jonas had been looking about her shop while she and I sat at her desk in the back. When we walked out, Jonas and I shook our heads, not knowing if it was more our imagination than reality.

The interview that has affected me most was with an articulate and talented ninety-year-old woman. Her life had been simple, she said, smiling effortlessly. She lived in Cleveland and for the previous twenty years she had been a sketch artist for certain newspapers and magazines. It had happened inadvertently, she added, shrugging her narrow shoulders, seemingly unimpressed with her success. She had been visiting the Cleveland Museum and had been struck by one of the paintings, a Sargent, *Portrait of Mrs. Ralph Curtis (Lisa de Wolfe Colt)*, and though she had seen it before, this time she was struck by profound sadness in the woman's expression. She took out her pad and began to sketch—she would do so from time to time with paintings she found compelling. As she spoke I pictured her standing before the Sargent with one leg forward—her stance when she had opened the door to greet me—looking up thoughtfully at the work then lowering her head to draw. An editor who worked for a city newspaper had walked by and had come over to look at her sketch. He nodded and suggested she come to his office the next day. That was the beginning, she said, crossing her hands on her lap.

She had one son who lived in California, the wine country, and her husband had been an exuberant person. Their relationship, she said, had been complicated—in some ways they had been opposites, had had different interests, but in other ways they had been very much alike.

A few weeks later, she sent a sketch of herself, a self-portrait so that I would remember her, and there was also a sketch of me, a smaller one—she apologized and said she tried to remember me as best she could, but the Sargent at the museum that had launched her career kept coming to mind instead. In the sketch of herself she appears as unimpressed with herself as she had in person, but her gaze is more focused, more penetrating than I remembered, and in her rendition of me I was surprised by my slightly lowered head, the furrow in my forehead, the intent expression and subdued sadness in my eyes. I have framed the sketch of her and it is in my small office; I look at it every day for inspiration and affirmation. She possessed no illusions; she was content.

Five months after we returned from the Riviera, a Saturday in mid-January—the first storm of the winter season, I believe—I had awakened late and Jonas had offered to make me breakfast in bed. As he generally did not like the snow, I was surprised by his animated mood. The window was clouded with white patches, sunlight piercing through;

I was happy to stay in bed, and remain beneath the warmth from the covering layers of blankets.

Jonas brought in the tray, smiling openly, no trace of irony. The aroma of bacon mingled with that of warm maple syrup was intoxicating. The snow was falling heavily now. I ate wholeheartedly; he sat on the edge of the mattress next to me, not saying a word, watching me closely.

When I finished eating, I lay back against the pillow and studied Jonas as if observing him through a different lens: his high forehead suggesting concern, his eyes small and brown, his lashes long, yet sparse, his face angular, his expression fixed. I was overcome by how much of an enigma he was to me.

He took the tray away and left the room. Soon he was standing in the threshold; he instructed me to close my eyes, his expression steadfast, half boy, half man. And I did so, firmly covering my lids with the palms of my hands, waiting in anticipation. I heard him call out, his voice hoarse with anticipation, telling me to wait, he wasn't quite ready. Finally he cried out, "Open!" I lifted my hands, and at first my gaze was blurred; but as my sight became clearer, I saw spread apart and taped on the wall across from the bed seven sketches—the ones I believed he had done in August, on the Riviera.

The first sketch was of bougainvillea, only bougainvillea, as if bursting from the wall, not the inspiring, richly colorful bougainvillea we admired each day, but now sketched in charcoal, mostly in black and white—hauntingly devoid of color. The starkness of this rendition was eerie to behold, more intricate and narrow, without bloom.

The second drawing was of Roberto Carini, sitting at a round white table, a smaller one, at the café part of the restaurant. One elbow on the table, his hand raised almost in a salute; he looks outward in profile, a hint of the sea in the distance, his expression is pensive, yet decisive.

The third one was of the man who nearly drowned, sitting on a small towel on a beach, in a bathing suit, his legs spread open, his wet hair pressed to his head like a skullcap. There is a sense of isolation in his demeanor and posture, his arms close, his shoulders, drooping.

The one next to it was a sketch of the Mediterranean Sea. Touches of gray throughout, and a narrow strip of sand outlines the shore, pebbles and rocks nearly covering it. Shadows darken the rocks and sand, the frothing waves overwhelmingly white.

The fifth work was of a lone palm tree, only the sky in the background, more white than gray. The dark fronds and even darker trunk appear ominous in contrast to the sky.

Next to it was one of Remy, Helen and Marc's child. He is dressed in the clothes he wore whenever he came down to dinner, a pressed short-sleeved shirt and shorts. In both hands he holds a small globe, cupping it as if fearful he may drop it, it seems. Behind him, in the distance, the sun is rising. His feet are bare.

The last one was of a young woman leaning forward against the railing of a balcony. The face is not visible. The nightgown she wears reveals much of her back. Her hair is in a French braid, falling to the middle of her spine. The sea is in the distance, and her arms are extended across the railing, her head is tilted to the left. Dangling from her right hand is what appears to be a postcard.

From time to time I will recall the winter morning Jonas presented me with the sketches. I understood it to be an affirmation of our relationship, an acceptance of himself, of me, of each of our flaws, ultimately of our marriage. He was exposing himself to me in a way he had not before. The sketches were piercing and revelatory. For in each work there was something of Jonas—his deep sense of irony in the sketches of the bougainvillea and the palm tree, his sense of fear in the one of Remy, his anguish that I had chosen the hotel on Eric's postcard for our honeymoon in the sketch of the young woman on the balcony, and that I had held on to the card. But it was clear we would go forward with our lives and not look back. At the same time I comprehended our path would not be smooth and easy, more prickly, not unlike the beaches of the Riviera.

It took me some time to summon my resolve—I prefer the word resolve to courage—to speak with my parents about their years in Trieste during the war. Five years after our return from our honeymoon on the Riviera, on a November day, with this purpose in mind, I went alone to visit them. I had been writing for the magazine for three years and had become adept at interviewing people. In my mid-thirties at the time, I was confident in my ability to ask questions subtly, yet thoroughly—I had honed my skills to a certain degree as an interviewer and journalist. Though I had not yet developed the necessary empathy, a professional empathy, you could say.

Jonas was busy with an upcoming exhibit, deciding which of his paintings he would choose, wanting to be true to the theme of what would be a broader showing of works by other artists as well. I told him I needed to see my parents as my father was not feeling well and it was difficult for my mother to care for him. He had had a virus and had not yet recovered from it. Although he was thin, he had a strong constitution so I was not concerned; yet he had recently turned seventy-five. I wanted to be certain he was not ignoring my mother's requests to consult his doctor if necessary.

When I arrived I was weary from the three-hour drive but not overly so, and spoke with my mother for a few minutes before going in to see my father. He was lying on his bed, watching the television. The Berlin Wall was coming down and he seemed amazed by it and appeared fully satisfied. I understood that he saw himself as a part of what had been accomplished. He was smiling steadily and I was reassured. In a way, given his past anti-fascist work, it was a gift to him, a reaffirmation of his beliefs, his hatred of oppression, his courage and selflessness.

I sat on the chair next to his bed and together we viewed the footage of the dismantling of the wall. Young men with large picks, chipping away at the wall, appearing lighthearted, more likely stunned by their newfound freedom. My mother soon came into the room; she sat on the bed and crossed her arms. She looked more tired than my father.

"Was it worth it?" she asked musingly.

My father looked sharply at her, and said, "Johanna, it is always worth it." She nodded and I noticed her eyes watering, but soon she composed herself.

She stood up and said she would start to make dinner.

I followed her out of the room and into the kitchen. I sat down at the table and crossed my legs, preparing myself to ask a question, one I'd most wanted an answer to since meeting Roberto Carini five years before.

My mother began to hum and when I offered to help her, she firmly shook her head. I went up to her and placed my hands on her shoulders; I realized she was crying. I guided her to a chair, then I pulled my seat close to hers, and leaned forward, looking directly into her eyes. I may have lacked the empathy I should have had, my gaze was perhaps too penetrating, but I needed to know the truth. "Why did Eric not speak when he was a child?" I asked, hearing a certain directness in my tone, one I had never used with her before. She was surprised by my question, taken aback; her defensiveness evaporated.

At first she spoke haltingly, searching for words, her eyes tear-filled, but soon her innate stoicism prevailed; her speech became succinct, her expression guarded. "He was with his sitter, they were walking down a dark street and heard screams; a woman Eric knew was being raped by two men who were angry with your father; they viewed him as a traitor, working for the other side. Eventually it was understood that Eric was mute for a few years because of what he had witnessed."

I was silent, stunned by her sense of dissociation. I knew to say no more, to not question her further.

The day before I left, my mother had driven to the store to pick up an item she had forgotten to purchase. It was the first time I had been alone with my father. He was much better by then, and was now watching the television in the living room, sitting in his favorite chair. He had been viewing the news almost continuously since the beginning of the fall of the wall. Growing up, I had known of no other person who was as humble and flexible as my father, and at the same time I realized that no one I had encountered was more resolute than he.

After my mother had walked out the door, I went to the front window and as I watched her drive away I felt chilled and hurt, fully comprehending that my life to a point because of my father's heroism had been formed by the violent actions of two men I did not know. But I grew to realize that both my mother and Eric had been much more affected than I had, an understanding that has become the basis of my compassion for Eric as well as for my parents. I now determined that the memory that had haunted me that summer and then suddenly lost its resonance, that eventually became insignificant, symbolized the underlying anguish of my mother and father during my youth. The memory lessened in strength not because it wasn't in one way or another true, figuratively or literally, but because I needed it to weaken in order to fully live.

Epilogue

Today is one of those late August days that occur sporadically during the last few weeks of the month; the sky is clear, the color of lapis, the leaves of a hickory are a resounding green, and the blue hydrangea in hue and form, at the height of its beauty, reflects the stately perfection of summer.

You decide to visit a gallery where one of your second husband's works is on display, a painting that evolved from a sketch he had done on the Riviera twelve years ago. When you walk in, the owner, a woman wearing black-framed glasses, her dark hair in a bun at the nape of her neck, is showing the painting to two customers, men in their mid-thirties. As you study a painting nearby, an abstract one with spurts of color, you overhear her words, her voice imbued with a dry fervency:

"The painting is by Jonas Smila-Hoffman. His work is a blend of postmodernism and traditionalism, though he says he does not like applying such labels to his paintings or to those of other artists. He is an interesting person, eclectic, in that he is not what he seems, though eventually one discovers most people are not. His paintings, muted in tone and color, are surprising, for they are essentially emotional and passionate, as is evidenced in this work, The Postcard. *How does he achieve this? It is his talent, I believe."*

Moving on to study another painting, you no longer hear her words, only the lull of her voice, followed by the questioning tones of the two men who are viewing it with her. Your mind wanders to the trip on the Riviera twelve years ago; you envision Jonas swimming fiercely and assertively, attempting to rescue the British couple. But after all this time, you have come to realize what he was doing was not trying to save the memory of Eric in your imagination as you first believed; instead he was hoping in some way to rescue your first husband, a fragment of his life itself, as if in doing so, the person he believed was complex, whom he admired and thought resembled the young woman in Botticelli's Primavera, *would return to him. No matter his reason, he had been brave to do so. For in the heat of a hazy August day, his motions were firm and clear. You recall what Helen's husband Marc later said, that Jonas, your second husband, was different than most.*

Though a circumstance may occur when you have the ability to be clear-eyed in the face of a seemingly impossible situation, rising above the heat and haze of it, reflecting the same sort of majesty that prevails on certain days in the last full month of summer. For in the midst of your deepest challenge, you may be selfless in choice or action, or, with all the strength you need to muster, walk away—whichever course you decide, at that moment, you are august.

www.ingramcontent.com/pod-product-compliance
Lightning Source LLC
LaVergne TN
LVHW090945080826
845145LV00003B/889

* 9 7 8 1 7 3 6 0 5 3 6 3 8 *